PRAISE FOR LAST DREAM OF HER MORTAL SOUL

"Koi, who can enter and manipulate other people's dreams, comes into her own in Lincoln's capable third urban fantasy...series fans will enjoy watching Koi learn to control her abilities and sort out her romantic life along the way."

—Publishers Weekly

PRAISE FOR THE PORTLAND HAFU SERIES

"DREAM EATER brings much-needed freshness to the urban fantasy genre with its inspired use of Japanese culture and mythology and its fully-realized setting of Portland, Oregon. I'm eager to follow Koi on more adventures!"

—Beth Cato, author of
The Clockwork Dagger and *Breath of Earth*

"In *Black Pearl Dreaming*, Koi is a delightfully watchable heroine in way over her head. She struggles to figure out whom to trust, where she can get good coffee, and what exactly she should do about this enormous sleeping dragon, in this fast paced paranormal intrigue set in a vividly detailed contemporary Japan."

—Tina Connolly, author of *Ironskin*
and *Seriously Wicked* series

Last Dream of her Mortal Soul

Portland Hafu, Book 3

K. Bird Lincoln

World Weaver Press

Published by World Weaver Press, LLC.
Albuquerque, New Mexico
www.WorldWeaverPress.com

Edited by Rhonda Parrish
Cover designed by Sarena Ulibarri.
Cover images used under license from Shutterstock.com.

First Edition March 2019
ISBN-10: 1-7322546-4-8
ISBN-13: 978-1732254640

Also available as an ebook.

DEDICATION

To the Rochester Fantastical Women (and especially J. Lynn Else & Krista Street for the NaNoWriMo challenge) for inspiring/pushing me to write more than I thought I could. Also to the protesters living in Portland: don't give up the good fight.

The Portland Hafu Series
Dream Eater
Black Pearl Dreaming
Last Dream of Her Mortal Soul
Bringer-of-Death (prequel novelette)

LAST DREAM OF HER MORTAL SOUL

CHAPTER ONE

I pounded a fist on the front door of Marlin's second-floor condo. No answer. Just like there had been no answer to my texts or Facetimes. If I had any clue about her condo neighbors, I'd have called them from Tokyo before we boarded the plane home to Portland. But of course, I'd avoided her neighbors the three years Marlin lived here—just as I avoided everyone to protect against accidental physical contact before I realized I wasn't actually a psychic freak, but the child of a dream eating Baku.

My sister always answered texts. Always. I hoped to god she was just angry at how little I'd communicated about Dad while we were in Japan and thus was giving me the revenge silent treatment. Considering alternatives would send me down a black hole of fears about the Kind—the creatures out of myth and legend Dad had neglected to inform me were my heritage. They had invaded my mundane life and turned everything topsy-turvy a month ago.

Ken had spent the entire plane ride home playing angsty, emo-boy in the window seat next to Dad. No doubt reconsidering his decision to abandon his long lifetime in Japan to follow me home. The last member of our strange quartet was also leaving behind his Tokyo home for a Portlander, but Pon-suma's calm, monosyllabic replies to my nervous chatter weren't nearly the life-ring I needed to keep from drowning in the sea of worry churning my insides. We'd come straight here from PDX at my insistence. Our luggage was still in the taxi. The boys crowded me in the narrow, open corridor. Thank God we'd left Dad in the cab or there wouldn't be room enough to breathe.

I pounded the door again and pushed the doorbell six times in a row.

"Not there. Or unable to answer," said Pon-suma in his usual unruffled, surfer-boy way.

"What do you mean unable to answer? Unable, like, dead?"

Ken, leaning elbows on the corridor's railing, looked over his shoulder at us. "No, that's not what he meant."

"I'm pretty sure there's no benign reason for not answering your door." My voice sounded shrill. Ken opened his mouth, and then snapped it shut. Good choice. He'd redeemed himself a bit from his obnoxious behavior in Japan, but he wasn't a hundred percent forgiven yet.

"Meter's running," said Pon-suma.

A muffled thud came from inside, followed by a giggle. Marlin's giggle. All my nascent worry morphed into a giant monster of raw irritation and I punched the doorbell ten times in quick succession. Pon-suma yawned and slipped a hairband from the medley on his left wrist, pulling back the tangled lengths of his caramel-dyed hair. I didn't even want to imagine what my own black mess looked like; transpacific flights were a bitch.

"Marlin, answer the damn door!" I yelled into the door's peephole.

There were some clicks and the ratchet of someone pulling the security chain from its slot. The door opened a crack. One eye— Pierce family hazel outlined in a ring of blue—peered out.

"Koi," Marlin said, her voice convincingly surprised. "Aren't you

2

in Japan?"

"Obviously I am not in Japan!"

A muffled voice behind her caused my sister to giggle. I flinched at the weirdness of Marlin, my super-organized, mothering, practical little sister giggling like an anime schoolgirl. "Not now," she said. Her eye disappeared, replaced by the back of her head. "It's my sister."

The door opened wider to reveal my entire sister in her fuchsia Turkish terrycloth bathrobe being embraced from behind by a skinny Thor look-alike with wet, slicked-back hair. Most of Thor Look-Alike's visible parts were naked. He wore only Union Jack boxers.

"Are you okay?"

Marlin barely glanced my direction. "Of course, I'm okay."

"You didn't answer my texts."

"Oh, sorry," said Thor. "That was my fault. I've been keeping Marlin…busy." His grinning, self-congratulatory expression left little doubt about what he meant.

Ooh. Yuck. TMI to the max. I drew back. No need to risk a dream fragment from an accidental brush of skin with Marlin's boytoy. I *so* didn't need to dream about him and my little sister tonight.

"She is unharmed," said Pon-suma. "Kwaskwi's text is urgent."

I flashed a flat palm in Pon-suma's face and addressed Marlin.

"Why didn't you answer my texts? Are you okay?"

"Oh yes," said Marlin in a throaty voice, "I'm definitely okay. I'd invite you all in, but the apartment's not decent."

Ken snorted. I gave him a death-glare. It wasn't funny. I was really worried on the plane when Marlin didn't answer texts or phone calls. Releasing an ancient dragon in Aomori, Japan and installing a rebellious Tokyo Hafu—the half-Kind in Japan who were revolutionizing the tradition-moribund institution that ruled all Kind in the Pacific Basin—onto the Tokyo Council had kept me off my own phone, so the irony of me being angry at Marlin for not

3

answering my texts didn't escape me. However, Kwaskwi's messages suddenly calling me home had been super cryptic and unhelpful. I knew the Portland Kind had been coming under attack, something terrible happened to his buddy, Dzunukwa, and people were connecting me to the whole mess because I kept going around and releasing dragons. Marlin was known to the Portland Kind as my sister. I didn't think anyone would go after her based on that, but what did I know? I hadn't even discovered I was Hafu through my Baku father until a few weeks ago!

"Let me introduce myself," said the man manhandling my baby sister, "I'm Pete." The arm he extended for a handshake was covered in intricate, full-sleeve tattoos the greenish-black of old ink. Inside the crowded pattern I picked out a raised white fist, the number 14 repeated, and a cross made of arrows. I stared at his hand. He gave a weirdly mirthful laugh.

"I'm Ken," said my Kitsune-not-quite-boyfriend-anymore. He inserted himself closer to the door to shake Pete's hand, lowering my risk of a skin brush with this guy.

"Are we good?" said Marlin. "Can I go get dressed now?"

I bit my lower lip. "There's stuff I have to tell you about Dad."

Marlin looked behind me. "He didn't come back home with you?"

"He did, but—"

"Then go away for a couple hours and give me a chance to get myself together." She cupped Pete's cheek with one hand and smiled. Her new manicure distracted me for a second. Marlin always went for bright and intricate patterns but usually tended towards floral and abstract art. Today her fingernails were painted a stark black. The white outline of a skull with four long teeth, reminding me vaguely of some Marvel superhero logo, grinned from each thumbnail.

"Marlin, please."

"Koi, I'm serious. See you later." No smile for me. She rolled her eyes and reached for the door handle, pulling it closed with more force than necessary.

"Forest Park," said Pon-suma in Japanese pointedly looking over the corridor railing at the waiting taxi van. "Kwaskwi threatens to send the Bear Brothers to escort us."

"Okay, okay."

Ken gave a little sigh. "*Daijyobu desu.* She's okay for now. Let's go find out what Kwaskwi wants and then we can come back."

I swallowed something bitter in the back of my throat. My stomach was still upset from the flight and some deodorant and a toothbrush were definitely called for soonish, but Ken was right. We needed to see what was upsetting Kwaskwi. I owed him a debt and he was calling it in. However, Dad was in the backseat of the van, more or less in a coma from dream-eating blowback, and I needed to make him comfortable at my apartment before gallivanting all around town at the beck and call of the Portland Kind's Siwash Tyee.

Pon-suma bounded down the metal staircase. Ken and I followed a little more cautiously in the light spring rain slicking the steps. Rhododendron petals from the overgrown bushes lining the path curled brown and sodden at the bottom. I directed the taxi driver the mile to my apartment nestled between a middle school field and a little shopping district that had no café. Ken paid the driver while Pon-suma helped me wrestle Dad out of the van.

Back in Japan, Midori showed me that although Dad's eyes remained closed, he gave no reaction to pinches or nudges, and prolonged skin contact showed me no dream fragments at all, he was not completely unaware. If you stood him up, his legs would just barely catch his weight so one person could slip an arm around his torso and move him without too much trouble.

We got him up the stairs of my apartment while Ken followed with our baggage. I'd lost most of mine during our Tokyo adventure, so there wasn't much. Pon-suma did an impatient shuffle while I fumbled for my key outside the familiar plain brown door. When I finally found it and put a hand on the knob, the door swung open.

Pon-suma instantly went into alert-dog mode. "Unlocked."

"Yes," I answered, my heart beginning to beat fast.

"Kennosuke-san," said Pon-suma.

Ken was beside me in a flash, face going Kitsune-feral. His normally warm brown eyes went dark-iris-on-dark-pupil black. The planes of his cheeks sharpened and he rested his weight on the balls of his feet. "I'll go first. Wait here, Koi."

It took only a few seconds, and then Ken was back, his Kitsune fierceness dialed back down to low. "No one's here now."

I handed Dad over to Pon-suma and pushed past him. My apartment was trashed. The curtains were shredded, along with Mom's Hawaiian flag quilt and a ton of paper was strewn across the floor. Cupboard doors hung off their hinges, smashed glass and shards of Marlin's hand thrown coffee mugs littered the kitchen.

"Oh, god," I breathed, a prickling shock crawling over my skin.

"Does this mean anything to you?" said Ken, tugging me into the bedroom. My dresser door hung open, clothing crumbled in a pile at the foot of my bed. The bed itself was weirdly still made with my Starry, Starry Night Van Gogh bedspread but someone had covered it in a uniform inch of what looked like flour. In the middle, something dark and syrupy and smelling of maple soaked the flour in an outlined symbol of three interlocking triangles. Underneath was a phrase in looping, erratic letters.

In that sleep of death.

CHAPTER TWO

I didn't immediately tell the boys that I recognized the phrase, or the fear the rest of that famous quote awoke in my middle. I held Dad's hands on the sofa, a light undercurrent of mixed awe and unease running through me at this fragment-less prolonged contact. His skin felt like brittle parchment and the veins bulged blue and gnarly on the back of his hands. He was getting old. It was the first time I thought he resembled the very old man he truly was.

Pon-suma got Dad to drink by using a turkey baster to sploosh water into his mouth and massaging his throat, but he told me sternly that we needed supplies to hook up Dad to an IV if he stayed unreactive.

I didn't want to imagine Marlin walking in here and seeing my mess of an apartment and Dad with a tube sticking out of his hand. It would be too close to what Mom looked like near the end of her cancer fight.

Ken tidied up a path through the living room to the kitchen by stuffing most of the floor mess into a trash bag.

"Thanks," I said as he hunkered down on his heels near where

Dad's head was resting on the cushions. He peered up at me through lush, fringed eyelashes that would have made most men look metrosexual androgynous, but only made Ken's dark gaze more primal, more deeply enticing.

"This was no meth-head looking for quick cash," said Ken. "It was a personal attack."

"Does that phrase on your bed mean anything to you?" Pon-suma asked in Japanese.

"I…I think it might be a Shakespeare quote."

The boys blinked at each other. Considering the amount of history they'd lived through, their unfamiliarity with classical literature was surprising. Then again, maybe I was being Anglocentric. I couldn't quote Murasaki Shikibu's *Tale of Genji*, and that was considered the first full-length novel ever written in the whole world. I'd learned that in Japanese lit class at PCC right before I'd met the murderous Professor Hayk.

"You can't stay here," said Ken.

The implications of the attack sifted through the distracting thoughts about literature and settled into my stomach like lead pellets. Someone had been in here, looking through my private stuff and shredding my underwear. Not that it was expensive or anything, but the malice in the person who'd touched all my things gave me the creeps. I didn't want to stay here and Marlin had company already.

"I don't have anywhere to go."

"Kwaskwi will put us up."

"I have no doubt Kwaskwi is going to put you up," I told Pon-suma, flashing back to the steamy lip lock Kwaskwi planted on Pon-suma when they said goodbye in Japan. "But I'm not sure that's entirely safe for me and Dad."

"She's right," Ken agreed. "Portland Kind are being attacked. The Herai Baku will only make Kwaskwi more of a target. We should go to a hotel."

I gulped. A hotel? For how long? I caught myself smoothing the back of Dad's hand with my thumb over and over again. Even though the Council had reimbursed me for part of the plane ticket, my bank account balance was dipping dangerously low from the Japan trip. Ignoring Portland Perlmonger gigs meant nothing got added back to that balance.

Kwaskwi and Ken never batted an eyelash at expenses, but there was no way in hell I would ask them for help. Besides, who knew what state Ken's finances were in? He'd quit his job as slave-assassin to the Tokyo Council when we released the Black Pearl from the Council's cave prison. He probably wasn't getting paychecks anymore, either. "I know the Rodeway Inn near the airport has cheap rooms."

Ken shook his head. "We need a suite. A hotel lobby provides another layer of security that a flimsy motel door does not." He scratched behind his ears with both hands, turning his artfully mussed short, black spikes into sleep tangles. "I'm thinking the Heathman Hotel."

I snorted. "The doorman's Beefeater costume just makes me giggle. But isn't that a bit too flashy? It's right downtown. Shouldn't we try to find a place a little more secluded? Or near to Kwaskwi?" I realized I didn't know exactly where Kwaskwi lived. Thunderbird, Kwaskwi's friend the ancient giant eagle, always flew home towards Mt. Hood. That meant west. "How about the McMenamin's Kennedy School Hotel? That's between the Pearl District and the airport, and not so chock full of tourist traffic."

Pon-suma pulled out his phone and swiped through a menu. He put the phone to his ear and switched to English for a quick greeting. "Koi's apartment was garbaged."

Pon-suma's colloquial English wasn't as good as Ken's. He continued explaining about my apartment, this time in Japanese. "I need a place to stay." He flicked his eyes over us and turned away, cupping a hand over his mouth and speaking in a low voice. Ken spoke to his back. "Don't tell Kwaskwi about our hotel."

When Pon-suma turned around there were twin pinpricks of pink high on his cheeks. Even this fierce Horkew Kamuy, which Ken had described as something like a dire wolf from the frozen tundra of Northern Japan, could blush. Especially when talking to a certain blue jay trickster.

"Kwaskwi is sending a car," Pon-suma said.

"It's safer if Kwaskwi doesn't know where the Herai are staying."

Pon-suma nodded and turned to me. "Two minutes. Do you need to pack?"

I gave a little laugh that came out half-sob. What would I pack? All my clothes were on the floor, ripped and ruined. The home invader had even trashed my closets. Nothing worth packing remained. Ken put an arm around my shoulder and squeezed. I let my head tilt, resting for a moment on his warmth and strength. "I'm good. Let's get Dad outside."

I texted Marlin that my apartment had been robbed, and that Ken and I were going to a hotel. Ken wouldn't let me tell her I'd gotten an online reservation for us at the Kennedy School. He was adamant no one should know. It felt like overkill, but then again, a sense of dread hung over me as I stood outside my apartment building, as if the dark clouds shrouding the Portland sky were more than just natural phenomenon.

The car appeared after ten minutes waiting in a light drizzle. I half expected a dark limo like the one the Council had us tooling around in back in Japan, but this was Portland. A green Subaru outback with a cedar canoe lashed to the top pulled up to the curb in a sudden, jolting stop. The passenger window rolled down and a familiar, burly round face framed by a bald top and bushy black beard, grinned out at me. An identical twin of that face sat at the wheel of the car.

The Bear Brothers. We'd met before when they were acting as Kwaskwi's bruisers trying to steal Dad away. We'd been at odds then. Now I suppose they were official colleagues since they were Kwaskwi's minions and I sort of trusted Kwaskwi. The passenger brother gave a slow nod of greeting. "Hello Koi Pierce." His voice was as growly and deep as you'd expect from a bear. "We have to take you to Forest Park."

The driver tapped him on the shoulder. A perplexed look came over the passenger. The driver whacked him across the back of the head. "Oh yes," said the passenger. "I'm supposed to introduce myself. Kwaskwi said it would make you less scared." He grinned wider, showing snaggle-teeth that had never seen braces. "We are Kwakwaka'wakw."

"Nice to meet you."

Driver whacked the passenger again. "The Kwakwaka'wakw are who we came out of, a Coast Salish people. It's hard to say. Sorry. Just call me Henry. The other one's George."

Ken gave a formal bow. "Fujiwara Ken." That was surprisingly close enough to his real, full name, that it made blink. Was making himself vulnerable to Kwaskwi's fellow Portland Kind a declaration of sorts of his intention to start over fresh?

Pon-suma did the same slow, grave nod as Henry. Apparently laconic Kind didn't need actual verbal introduction. Or maybe Kwaskwi had already let slip his new main squeeze's details.

The boys got Dad into the back of the car and Ken and I squeezed in on either side of him. Pon-suma slid into the front seat next to the passenger Bear Brother where he immediately was dwarfed by Henry's bulk. Henry was definitely the chatty brother of the two. He was like a big, bald elderly aunt starved for company. All the small talk directed at Pon-suma was met with his trademark succinct answers. This didn't faze Henry. He twisted around in the front seat and peppered questions at me while his twin maneuvered like a getaway driver to get us onto the highway in record time.

"How was Japan?'

"It was interesting."

"I've never been to Japan, I've always wanted to go, but whenever Kwaskwi leaves Portland he says to me and George that we have to

11

hold down the fort in case someone gets cranky. Of course we've visited with Aello and Ocypete in New York. Wow, that was the best baklava I've ever had. But unless you count Canada as international, and really, who does, then I've never been outside the U.S." And so on and so on. I'd been so scared of them before, it was laughable.

My heart lifted as we neared the Burnside Bridge. Mt. Hood rose up over the White Stag sign and that feeling of home truly clicked into place, but by the time we reached the Thurman Street Bridge and parallel parked, my face had frozen into a vacant smile. Ken's eyebrow had a permanent arch of amusement. George cleared his throat when the car stopped and Henry stopped his titillating recitation of the menu from his birthday dinner bash at Le Pigeon. "Kwaskwi's waiting under the bridge." He concluded and then went weirdly silent, obviously expecting us to jump right out of the Subaru.

"I'll stay with Dad while you go see what he wants," I told Ken.

Ken shook his head. "He wants you."

Pon-suma patted Henry's shoulder. "Kwaskwi said you keep us safe, yes? This is Herai Akihito. You watch over him."

Henry spluttered "But the Siwash Tyee told us—"

George reached his hand past his brother to grasp Pon-suma's. They gave each other an involved fist-bump handshake and did a double grave nod. *The bear to the wolf: that's settled.*

Dad was still unconscious but otherwise fine. Still. "I can't just leave him here." I regretted not leaving him with Marlin. I could be walking into danger. Caught between a rock and hard place I pressed knuckles into my eye sockets.

"I give my word," said Henry, querulous aunty demeanor settling into solemn regard. "George and I will defend him to the death."

God we were being dramatic. Kwaskwi was the leader of the Portland Kind, and these two were his friends. It wasn't like I was abandoning Dad at the side of the road. "Thank you," I said. Henry had such a hang dog face, I gave in to the uncharacteristic urge to

12

squeeze his arm through his jacket. I held up a finger. "Just one moment." I dialed the number of the adult day care we'd used sometimes when both Marlin and I were busy.

Nurse Jenny answered on the third ring. I negotiated temporary respite care for this week while Henry listened intently. Nurse Jenny drove a hard bargain, but finally admitted there was an open bed. Hopefully Marlin would help pay for this since she was so busy with…her own stuff.

"Can you take Dad to this address?" I flashed Henry the Google map on my phone. Henry grabbed the phone and showed it to George who looked thoughtful for a moment. He nodded.

Henry grinned. "Be back in two shakes of a lamb's tail." He looked too young to talk like a ninety-year-old Midwesterner but who knew how old the Bear Brothers actually were. I knelt on the backseat and kissed Dad on the cheek. "You are safer with Nurse Jenny," I said. "Forgive me for this."

Ken tugged me out of the car and I watched the Subaru drive away. It felt like something important was missing, like I'd misplaced my keys or lost my phone. There was nothing to do but get Kwaskwi's summons over with as soon as possible.

Pon-suma led us along the street to the staircase inset on a small incline near the bridge. We filed down the stairs and into McLeay Park, a small green hollow bordered on both sides by lush thickets. Streetlights, the tops of houses, and electrical lines skimming over the treetops just barely invaded the natural quiet of the space. We were only a few blocks from the trendy restaurants and bustling foot traffic of the Pearl District, but it felt like we weren't in the city at all.

Something chittered above and I looked up to see a band of blue jays lining the Thurman Street Bridge's metal rail, every single one of them turned sideways so one beady black eye fixed on us.

"Took your time," said a female voice. Startled, I gave a little jump. The jays shifted and fluffed their wings, chortling to each other.

"Elise," I said, recognizing the blonde cheerleader-type in a pale blue track suit lurking in the dry shadows underneath the bridge support. She gave us a narrow smile, her perfect teeth a slice of flashy white, and flipped a sleek ponytail over one shoulder.

Pon-suma looked expectantly at me. *Guess I'm doing the introductions.*

"Elise, you remember Ken. This is Pon-suma. He's from the Tokyo Kind." I left off his nature as well as the rest of his name. I wasn't going to make that mistake again.

"Tokyo Hafu," Pon-suma corrected. He nodded at Elise.

Elise's smile became thoughtful. "Oh, I know who you are. *What* you are. Kwaskwi's a terrible gossiper."

I sighed. Kwaskwi wasn't here. He must be somewhere up one of the paths. I was hoping this would be a quick thingie, so I could check in with Nurse Jenny about Dad, get a room at the hotel, and grab an honest-to-god barista handcrafted latte from Stumptown. I'd even settle for driving through Dutch Brothers and facing one of their way too chipper young hotties. Jet lag like cotton muffling slowed the speed of my thoughts.

"This way," said Elise, ducking out from under the bridge into the drizzle.

Nope, no latte in my immediate future. She headed towards an unmarked footpath at the bottom of the steepest part of the hill. There were only two trailheads at Lower McLeay Park, the one she chose wasn't the short one to Pittock Mansion. Just my luck. Instead of coffee, I got a long hike through rainy woods up into Forest Park and the site of an alleged passion killing: The Witch's Castle.

CHAPTER THREE

The jays catapulted into the sky, wheeling left, right and then disappearing into the hilltop trees in a jabbering cloud.

"The Bear Brothers will do fine with Dad, right?" I said quietly. We walked single file while Pon-suma and Elise forged ahead.

"Who?" Ken gave me a confused look.

"George and Henry."

"Pon-suma invoked Kwaskwi's hospitality. That's a sacred trust." We both spoke Japanese, carving out a small slice of intimacy under the eerie quiet of the trees and Elise's unsettling presence. Not that I could be sure she didn't speak Japanese. I mean, I'd met her the first time in Kaneko-sensei's Japanese Lit class at Portland Community College. Kwaskwi had already showed he was fluent and literate in Japan. I shouldn't make assumptions.

"What if he wakes up? What if he is confused and scared?"

Ken gave me a measured, careful look. His how-much-can-Koi-handle gauging looks made me crustier than day old baguette but even I could hear the whining rise to my voice. I wanted to blame lack of sleep and lattes, but the reality was my fear for Dad was easier to handle than whatever Kwaskwi wanted at the Witch's Castle.

"What Herai-san did, what you did together in Aomori to release the Black Pearl, was a major working, even for the most powerful Kind like Baku. Those workings take a major release of energy, the kind you only get from death or birth. He should be dead."

I gasped. His words were a hot needle slipped under my breastbone. The reason we were alive was because a snow woman on the Tokyo Council, Yukiko, had given her life instead. But Dad was not entirely okay. I couldn't lose him. "Are you saying the coma is permanent?" In my distress I stopped in the middle of the path.

Elise flashed us an exasperated glance.

"He might wake up," said Ken. "But it won't be today."

"We gotta hoof it. There's a time limit here," Elise said.

We resumed our march into the twilight quiet of the forest. Pon-suma broke off to circle a downed tree blocking the dirt path. My foot caught on an exposed root, and I stumbled. Ken grabbed my arm and steadied me, the brief flash of warmth welcome against the dreariness of the weather and my fears.

"There better be St. Honore croissant at the end of this hike," I grumbled as we waded through ferns adorned with droplets of water that soaked a bone-chilling damp through my cotton leggings.

"Of course, Koi knows where the nearest bakery is," muttered Elise.

"It's like she has bakery-dar," said Ken. No one laughed.

"Okay, wait here," said Elise, jogging a few steps to catch up with Pon-suma. He stopped and stood motionless.

"Kwaskwi's right over there," said Pon-suma, his chin indicating a stand of tall cedars.

"Look who has Kwaskwi-dar," I said under my breath.

Ken arched an eyebrow in amusement, but Pon-suma just looked puzzled. Yep, his English definitely was not as good as Ken's.

Elise clucked her tongue in impatience. "There's a circle of protection. We have to wait for Kwaskwi to let us through."

The band of jays from the bridge materialized over the tree canopy and dropped like blue fluff bombs forming a curved line on the pine-needle covered ground. I became aware of a curious hum, a current of energy-laden sound halfway between a moan and a wooden flute's shrill. The birds chortled and jostled each other while the sound intensified, making my wisdom teeth vibrate. Ken put a hand to his forehead, digging a thumb into the sensitive hollow under his ear. Then, with a curious pop, the sound stopped and the birds went still, standing at attention like porcelain figures.

Elise stepped over the line of birds and waved us forward.

"What is that?"

Ken gave me a grave look. "Not something usually practiced during daylight hours in public. Kwaskwi must have a good reason to be so blatant about keeping people out of this area."

I stepped over the jays. They remained deathly still until we'd all crossed over, then they exploded in all directions, only to bunch together in a churning mass of wings, feathers, beaks, and loud cawing that rose like a balloon. The ball of living jays solidified, morphed together in a dark mass, and disappeared behind a tall cedar with bushy upper branches.

A man dropped eight feet down from the top of the cedar. He was clad in a red plaid shirt under a creased and worn black leather jacket sporting silver chains. His jeans were more workman than fashion, and his black cowboy boots sported inlays in an intricate pattern of blue feathers, arrows and leaves. He stood up from a crouch and dusted pine needles from his knees.

Kwaskwi. The Siwash Tyee of the Portland Kind, which I had finally found out from Ken meant something like leader. He did not give his usual wide horse-like grin. He was serious. Somber. Utterly unlike the man I'd come to rely on for providing a wake-up dose of levity during the overly-dramatic Kind hoopla.

"Come," he said, turning heel and striding uphill back on the hiking path.

Wow. No greeting. No nod even for Pon-suma. My estimation of the situation's probable horror ratcheted up a notch.

Ken took my elbow, steering me towards the path when I hesitated to follow. Usually I found manhandling irritating, but I was comforted by his closeness even though he'd lost my unreserved trust after the way he'd betrayed me to the Council. And hidden the fact that while playing slave-assassin he was really working for the release of the Black Pearl along with The Eight Span Mirror—the rebellious Hafu Kind in Japan. Apparently sensitive information like that wasn't safe with me. Not sure how a man who claimed to care could deem me so useless.

Since his attempt at self-sacrifice—to provide the kind of death energy necessary for the Black Pearl's release—was foiled by Yukiko, he'd become quiet and reserved. Many things boiled underneath that reserve, though, I knew. His angst level was high now that he had no mission to focus on.

I felt the pressure of his measuring gaze on me more than ever, taking things in, weighing all his words, and processing things as if everything was new and uncharted territory. Which, I supposed, it was. He hadn't expected to be alive past the release of the Black Pearl. But he was. And now he had to figure out what that meant.

Kwaskwi stopped on the path just below the Witch's Castle. It was a ramshackle, crumbling four-room stone building missing most of a roof. Its inside walls were covered in layered graffiti and outside walls were green with creeping vines. Everyone said it was haunted.

Back in 1850, or so the story went, a man hired an itinerant worker to help him clear land. The worker fell in love with the man's daughter, married her against the man's wishes and fled. One night, the man came upon the couple and shot the itinerant worker dead. The man himself was hanged in 1859 in what is widely considered Oregon Territory's first legal hanging. Until his death, the man swore his own wife had witched him into the murder. The wife lived in the house for years after—thus the name Witch's Castle.

"Come." Kwaskwi's resonant voice was sharp with impatience. When everyone moved forward, he brandished an open palm. "No, only Koi. By the debt you professed to me at Ankeny Square, I bid you."

Ken's eyes widened. "There's no need to be this formal, unless—"

"Unless what?" I knew this wasn't going to be a walk in the park. "I can handle it. Kwaskwi won't let anything harm me."

"Are you sure? You are not his people, Koi."

"I'm not Tokyo's either. Still. He's my friend."

"Am I not also your friend?"

My feet propelled me up the path. Large bags hung under Kwaskwi's eyes. Pine needles studded his long shiny, dark hair. "You look tired," I said.

"You look like crap," he countered.

"Transpacific flights don't agree with me and I didn't even stop for food. Neither you nor Marlin were answering your phones. I went to Marlin's apartment first."

"Is she all right?"

"Shacked up with some guy I've never met, but okay."

"Good," said Kwaskwi.

We arrived at the bottom of the moss-covered staircase leading up the side of the structure. Kwaskwi took each step one at a time as if he were burdened with some heavy load.

"Are you all right?"

He beckoned me up the stairs. "I've kept up a circle of protection around this area for 48 hours. I'm about to drop. If you would just *hustle* that Yankee girl ass then I can rest."

And there's the Kwaskwi I know and love. I jogged up the rest of the stairs, too tired to drum up a clever comeback. And then, faced with the understanding of why Kwaskwi wasn't completely his usual self, I stopped dead at the top of the stairs.

Spread eagled on the cold stone floor was a familiar figure. Dzunukwa, the Ice Hag. She'd first accosted me in Pioneer Square three weeks ago, blowing her ice wind through me when Ken and I were trying to reach Kwaskwi's designated meeting space on time or risk losing Dad to him. She'd terrified me then. All red, red lips, tangled bird's nest of hair, and a multicolored gypsy skirt inlaid with polished children's teeth that flashed like mirrors. Even more terrifying, I'd used my Baku dream eating as a weapon for the first time on her—a living, waking being. Reveling in the power, repulsed by my own hunger, I'd almost drained her dry.

Now she lay here, her hair fanned out around her head like a dark starburst. Dead. Her lips were pursed as if about to send a stream of heart-stopping cold, but her black eyes were open, staring, and lifeless. Someone had carefully arranged her skirt so it spread wide, and placed her arms across her middle in a terrible mimicry of a ballerina's first position. My mind yawned wide, a formless void. There was no comprehending what my eyes beheld. She was here, murdered. And above her on the stone wall was the rest of the Shakespeare quote someone had painted in maple syrup on my bed. Only here it was traced in something dark-red, crumbling, and smelling of sour melon and pennies.

What dreams may come?

CHAPTER FOUR

Kwaskwi folded his arms and regarded me with impatience. "This quote means what to you?"

"It's not my quote!"

"It means something to you, baby Baku. Whoever did this," he gritted his teeth, narrowing his eyes further and taking a deep, deep breath through his nose, "is calling you out."

From this sleep of death, what dreams may come. What he said made sense but every cell in my body revolted at the idea of having any responsibility for this awful death. I couldn't admit to this serious, scary Kwaskwi what was written in my apartment. "It's a Shakespeare quote."

"Hamlet, yes I know. Dzunukwa was killed and left here for the Portland Kind to find as a message. It has nothing to do with Hamlet, and probably everything to do with dream eaters."

I shook my head, tears welling from my left eye. I wiped at it with the back of my hand. "I swear to you, Kwaskwi, I have no idea how or why this happened. I've been in Japan for the last week! You were there with me."

"Yes," said Kwaskwi gravely. "And me vouching for you is the only reason the rest of the Portland Kind aren't calling for your blood." He hunkered down on his heels and rested his face in his palms. "Dzunukwa was murdered while I was gone." His shoulders shook, and I heard the raspy, stuttered breathing of someone holding back sobs. "I should have stayed here."

I put my hand on his shoulder, the leather cold and damp under my palm. "What can I do to help? I'll do whatever I can, but I can't," I swallowed bile, "I can't eat the dreams of a dead person." At least I didn't think I could. Dad had never mentioned this possibility and no way did I want to find out by touching Dzunukwa. *Do the dead dream?*

Kwaskwi looked up at me. "You agree to help?" His eyes were clear, his voice bright with eagerness.

"What can I do?"

"You'll do whatever you can?"

"I said I would!"

"That's what I needed to hear," he said, standing up so suddenly I stumbled backwards. "Three times."

Oh crap. Saying something three times was in like all the fairy tales from a bunch of different cultures. It was so hard to keep up with this stuff through jet lag and hunger. "What did I just get myself into?"

Kwaskwi stepped around Dzunukwa's corpse and entered the Witch's Castle through the door set into the triangular wall. I followed, my heart beating too fast. There was more? This part of the house was roofless, and open to the elements. Kwaskwi walked to the other side, where a shorter staircase wound down the side of the house to the first floor. Missing a wall on only one side, the first floor was a shadowed large room smelling of damp, mulch and Axe Body Spray.

I coughed, peering into the darkness of the far corner. A white guy about my age was huddled in the corner on the floor with his arms wrapped around his bent knees. Only shorts and a red Make America Great Again! T-shirt protected him against the chill. His fingertips pressed so hard into his knees that the nail beds were white and bloodless.

The tip of a blue feather poked from his closed lips.

"Who is this? Did he…is this the person who did that to Dzunukwa?"

"No, not him." Kwaskwi stepped closer to the guy. Although he didn't try to get up or run away, Kwaskwi's presence clearly terrified him. His chest rose and fell rapidly, hyperventilating without a sound.

Dread moved in and made itself at home low and heavy in my belly. I closed my eyes for a second, not wanting to see. Not wanting to be here at all. Blundering around with magical Kind and their otherworldly politics was one thing. This was messy and terrible and human. The guy in the corner was going to send me further along the haunted path of no return, I could feel it.

When I opened my eyes, Kwaskwi beckoned me with a single, curled finger. "You offered to help three times."

I was pretty sure that three times thing was bullshit, but it wasn't like I could confirm that with Ken or Pon-suma. Besides, Kwaskwi *was* my friend. I settled on my heels next to the guy. His eyes didn't track. They stayed fixedly staring into space over Kwaskwi's head. "Hey there," I said softly.

No reaction.

"I'm not going to be much help getting him to talk if he's gagged."

Kwaskwi leaned down. "It's not talking that you're here for."

"How long have you kept him like this?'

"I found him poking around the border of my circle yesterday. He saw something when Dzunukwa was attacked."

I spread my hands, balancing uncertainly in my squat. "And you couldn't just ask him? This is what you do to a witness?"

Kwaskwi looked down at me, the hardness of his resolve softening into pity. As if I were a naïve fool who still believed monsters didn't live under the bed. "A witness who did not call the police. Who stood by while a woman was brutally murdered."

"Dzunukwa is not by any stretch of the imagination normal. What could a regular old human do when confronted with all...this? To run screaming in the opposite direction is the *normal* reaction."

"Don't let your prejudice against Dzunukwa blind you to the sanctity and value of her life. All life is precious, even an Ice Hag's."

"This guy's life is precious!"

The guy gave a low whimper. Kwaskwi shook himself, letting the scary intensity melt into the relaxed *aw shucks* persona that didn't fool me anymore. "He'll be okay. You do your Baku thing, get me a clue who did this, and we'll let him go with a dose of Elise's special Compazine-Zoloft cocktail to make this all feel like a bad dream."

"This doesn't feel right."

Kwaskwi gave an exasperated sigh. "The faster you get dream-eating, the faster this young man can go."

I stood up. "This is not on me. Even if I touched him there's no guarantee that I would even see a memory dream. I'm more likely to get a fragment about being naked in class or flying over the Willamette."

"I have faith in the Baku who has released two ancient dragons from their prisons. I need you to find who did this. Leaving Dzunukwa to the human police is not an option. Help me, Koi AweoAweo Pierce. Help all of us."

He'd used my full name. A physical tug on my heart made me gasp, as if his voice reached into my rib cage like a fishhook. I wanted to help him. The sight of Dzunukwa on the stones ate away my sense of home and safety. It was just wrong. She was a powerful, vital being and something or someone had stopped her life as if it were worthless, a plaything to be used and discarded. If I could do something to stop that person from hurting anyone else, I needed to.

But not this. Not forcefully dragging a dream from some human guy whose biggest sin was blundering into Kind politics at Forest Park. What if this was Ed? Or Craig-ever-chipper the Stumptown Barista, or Marlin? Forcefully ripping a dream from a human would drain them of essential life force. It was the worst kind of invasion. No, this wasn't a line I could cross and still live with myself.

"I'm sorry, Kwaskwi. I can't."

"You have to." The angry squawking of jays arose in the trees around the house. The guy gave a sea lion's gagging cough. Feathers dark with saliva and bile erupted from his mouth as his eyes widened with terror.

"He's choking!"

Kwaskwi curled his hands into fists, piercing me with an obsidian gaze. "You owe me a debt!"

And then Ken was there standing beside me in feral Kitsune mode, lithe, muscular, breathing hard in a fighting stance. "Back down," he said quietly.

"She has to find out who did this!" Kwaskwi reached for my arm, but Ken was faster, inserting himself between us just in time.

"You risk breaking her!" Ken deflected Kwaskwi's arm with a downward elbow jab, following through with the motion so that his shoulder ended up under Kwaskwi's armpit for a judo-style throw. But Kwaskwi drew himself up out of the arm lock and spun backwards.

"You refuse this?"

Tears welled, hot and blurry. It was one thing using my dream eating on Kind who threatened me, it was another to use it on an innocent human. I couldn't do it, no matter how much Kwaskwi yelled. No matter if a hot mantle descended on my shoulders and back at the idea of disappointing him, of failing again. "Let me help another way."

Kwaskwi's breathing was harsh in the damp quiet. "You are not released from this debt." He spoke to me despite his full death glare battle with Ken. The testosterone level was so intense that I could smell it.

The guy had finished gagging. Streaks of vomit and feathers stained the front of his shirt, pooling between his feet. I patted him on his back as his coughing receded. "What's your name? I'm Koi."

Kwaskwi hissed in disapproval. Okay, so maybe telling him my name wasn't the smartest move of the century, but how else was I supposed to break the ice? The guy was terrified.

"What do you want with me? I don't have much money but it's yours!" The guy reached behind him as if to pull out a wallet.

"No, no, it's okay," I said, trying to pull the corners of my mouth into something resembling a smile. It must have been more gruesome than I'd intended because he blanched and froze.

"Don't do that…choking thing, please."

I glared at Kwaskwi. *Look what you did. Scared a poor harmless guy.* But no, this guy had seen Dzunukwa die and not called the police. I wasn't willing to force a dream out of him, but we could still ask questions. "Ken," I said. "Make yourself into an encyclopedia salesman."

"*Nani ichatteru wakaranai.*" The Japanese male version of *what the hell are you saying girl?*

"No one's going to make you choke again," I said. "We're not dangerous."

The guy gave a little sob.

I made a hurry up motion with my hand at Ken, switching to Japanese. "Look harmless. Tone down the rabid Kitsune look."

Ken arched an eyebrow at me in his arrogant Spock way, but his features softened. Cheekbones rounded, eyes became wider and set further apart. His pouty lower lip widened into a generous smile. Kitsune magic, illusion that Ken had used on me countless times when he wanted me to trust him.

"Help me get him up," I said to Ken. Kwaskwi glowered at us from the corner.

When we got him standing, I took a step back. "Look…ah…dude," I paused waiting for him to fill in his name.

"Brian," he mumbled.

"Brian. We know you were here when that woman was attacked. We just want to know what you saw. Who was it?"

Brian glanced at Ken, bracing himself as if he expected a blow, and when nothing was forthcoming, looked down at the floor.

This wasn't working. "We will let you go if you just answer some questions. You can say yes or no, right? Who hurt that woman? Was it a man?"

Brian jerked back against the cold stone. "I didn't say that. I didn't say nothing! They said they'd kill me if I talked."

"Who?" Ken demanded. "Who will kill you?"

"You won't trick me. I won't snitch. It's them or us. Them or us. Blood and soil."

"What is he talking about?" said Ken.

"This is what happened before," said Kwaskwi. "That's why I needed Koi. He just jabbers on and on about this nonsense."

"Them or us," I repeated.

Ken went into non-threatening mode, relaxing his shoulders down, leaning weight on one leg, crossing his arms in front like he needed the protection. "Us, we choose us, right Brian?"

Brian's mouth shut with an audible click of teeth. He shivered. "Let me go, please just let me go."

"Let's get out of here, Brian. Before those bad men come back," said Ken.

Kwaskwi gave a little snort. I waved a hand in front of his face to shush him.

Ken's Kitsune illusion of softness was having an effect on Brian. His breathing had slowed, and he looked at Ken with hope. "I can go?"

"We'll go together."

But Brian wailed, clenching his fists, screwing his eyes shut.

Slamming his head back and forth he punched wildly at Ken. I scooted back, mouth hanging open in surprise.

"No! No! You're one of them. One of *them*. Like that freaky old hag. You're lying. Let me go!"

Brian made a break for it but Kwaskwi caught him around the middle before he'd taken three steps. Brian went limp in his arms, sobbing. "Let me go. Let me go."

"Who was it?" Kwaskwi shook Brian so hard the guy's teeth rattled.

"The wolves! The wolves. I swear I only saw them."

Kwaskwi's grip loosened in surprise. "Wolves?"

"Nordvast Uffheim," Brian sobbed and then shot away like an arrow.

"He's getting away!" said Ken, poised to race after him.

"It's okay," said Kwaskwi. He took a deep breath. "Let him go," he yelled towards the bottom of the staircase where Elise stood, a pale figure in her powder blue track suit under the shadows of ancient cedars.

"You know these wolves? What was he talking about? I've never heard of wolf Kind here in the Pacific Northwest," said Ken.

"Not Kind," said Kwaskwi. He stared a challenge at me, lifting his chin as if daring me to stop the next words. "Human. Human scum killed Dzunukwa."

CHAPTER FIVE

Kwaskwi lifted Dzunukwa from her sprawled position, tenderly clasping her against his chest. Blood stained his jacket, but that didn't seem to matter. Tears streamed down from eyes squeezed tightly against a grief so enormous it shimmered in the air. He mourned Dzunukwa the same way I would mourn Dad or Marlin. As if she were family. I'd only known her as a creepy Ice Hag, an enemy, but she'd been part of something, the Portland Kind, and it was clear how deeply that loss cut Kwaskwi.

He walked slowly down the path to where Elise waited. She hung her head as Kwaskwi passed. The line of birds beyond the path took off, gathering on the wall above my head. Eerily silent, they stared at Ken and me with all the haughty arrogance of wild predators eyeing a treat.

"We should go," I said, backing down the path. Ken followed.

As soon as we moved, the jays dive-bombed the area stained with blood and graffiti, coating it in a white layer of excrement.

"Effective deterrent for human forensics," Ken said.

"So gross."

Pon-suma fell in last, implacable and stoic as ever I'd seen him. We formed a silent funeral procession back towards Lower McLeay Park until the bridge's metalwork glinting in the late afternoon sun emerged through the trees. Kwaskwi went up the staircase with Dzunukwa and returned without the body or his leather jacket. *Red plaid is a great color for people around murders.* This was the Survivalist part of myself, trying to process the horror into something bearable. Morbanoid Koi was too despondent to speak up at all.

"We've got a lead," Kwaskwi told Elise.

"Koi did her thing?"

"No," he said. "She still owes me a debt."

Elise rolled her eyes. "What's the problem, Koi. Cold feet? Grow a pair."

Her disdain stunned me into silence. I fumed. *Where does Little Miss Cheerleader get off judging me? Like she does anything to help except skulk around and spy!* What the hell was Elise anyway? She did nothing that I could see as Kind-like other than hang out with Kwaskwi.

"Are you afraid of that man telling the authorities?" Ken asked. "You didn't give him drugs."

Kwaskwi shook his head. "I'm not too worried. He didn't go to the police before, and now he'll be terrified of being connected with us at all."

Ken repeated the strange phrase Brian had yelled. "No rad vast? Urufuhaimu?"

"Nordvast Uffheim," Pon-suma corrected. "Swedish. Northwest Wolfhome."

This was the first thing he'd said since the Witch's Castle. Kwaskwi swung around, appraising him from head to toe as if noticing him for the first time. Pon-suma stood his ground, giving no quarter, no flicker of emotion.

Something clicked into place. "I've heard that on the news. Isn't that the Skin Head group that claimed responsibility for the graffiti and vandalism at the Islamic Center of Portland last year?"

Kwaskwi nodded. "I keep tabs on all armed groups in the area. That's one I've had an eye on for a long time."

"You think Brian is Neo-Nazi?" Pale and pathetic Brian didn't seem like the type.

"Neo-Nazis would slam you for calling them Skin Heads," said Elise. We all looked at her.

"What? I did a paper on them for a PCC sociology class last semester."

"Doesn't matter what Brian is. He has no taint of Dzunukwa's blood on him," said Ken.

"You can smell that under all that cologne?"

Ken dismissed my comment, starting for the stairs. "The Siwash Tyee is done with us for now. We can go."

Kwaskwi's upper lip curled in a sneer. "Who's this *us* you talk of? It's Koi that owes me a debt. There is no obligation between us, Bringer." The sneer turned into a toothful grin. "Unless you have plans to offer fealty to the Portland Kind now that you're a free agent?"

"The mistakes I make now will be my own," said Ken. "I am done accumulating sin for anyone. I'm here with Koi."

Well gosh. Lay it out there for everyone and their mother to hear. I didn't need the Siwash Tyee or Ms. Cheerleader up in my business. "I'm exhausted. If you need us, Ken and I will be at the Kenne—"

Ken clapped a hand over my mouth. "Just text her."

Kwaskwi's generous mouth curled up at the sides, a pale ghost of his usual wide grin. "You're dismissed." He made a shooing motion. Then, as Pon-suma began climbing the stairs behind us, he coughed in a theatrical way. "Not you, shrine boy."

Kwaskwi went to Pon-suma, gripping him about the shoulders and settling his forehead against the other man's, touching noses. "Joy in my heart to see you brother," he said in a barely audible tone.

Elise suddenly found her Sketchers utterly compelling and Ken turned half away, as if that would give them privacy. I stuck my tongue in the middle of his palm and he dropped it from my mouth with a shudder, wrinkling his nose. He backed up, wiping his hand on a pants leg. *Not how you reacted to my tongue before.*

Pon-suma was stiff but as Kwaskwi maintained a firm grip, he slowly softened. A sigh escaped one of them. "Distant may the path be that takes me away again."

Kwaskwi answered in an unfamiliar language. It sounded like the same language Pon-suma had used in the Black Pearl's cave when he was saving my bacon from the giant dragon's thrashing tail. The effect on Pon-suma was instantaneous. He turned bright red.

I swallowed a completely inappropriate giggle.

Ken elbowed me in the rib.

"Ow."

"Let's go."

At the top of the stairs, George and Henry were sitting in the grass on overturned paint cans smoking identical corncob pipes. A haze of pepper, sage and eucalyptus surrounded them. Henry cupped the bowl of his pipe in his left hand and withdrew it from his mouth. "You'll have to call Lyft or something. The Siwash Tyee commandeered the Subaru for Dzunukwa. We're just waiting for him to get up here and then we'll take them to—"

George put a meaty hand on his brother's knee. Henry and I were apparently vying for most blabber-mouthed today. Smoke seeped into my throat. I gave a little cough.

"Sorry. It's kind of a purification thing, you know," said Henry. He took a deep breath, obviously about to launch into another spiel, but this time Ken clicked his heels together, gave a low bow, and grabbed my shirt-elbow. "Thank you for your service. We will no longer impose on your hospitality." He dragged me a few feet down the sidewalk, the opposite direction from St. Honore.

"That way is coffee and sanity," I said, pointing back the way we came. Ken rolled his eyes. He took the precaution of crossing to the other side of the street before returning the way we'd come. Henry stood and gave us a vigorous wave as we passed.

"Seriously," Ken muttered.

"Don't be so grumpy. He's cute. And refreshingly chatty."

Ken tugged on my sleeve to drag me closer. He bent down so his lips were close to my ear, bathing me in his breath's bitter, *kinako*-cinnamon that set off really, really inappropriate reactions up and down my spine. "You can't afford to be naïve, here. Things are too dangerous. George and Henry are berserkers. They are not teddy bears."

"Okay, okay," I wrenched my arm away, rubbing my shoulder. "But they're also Kwaskwi's people. There's no reason to think they'll jump out and attack us. Also, we are stopping for a coffee and treats at St. Honore before we go to Kennedy School Hotel."

"Sure," said Ken. "I know better than to get between a Koi and her latte, but we'll need to find another hotel. Pon-suma heard us say that one."

"Now you don't trust Pon-suma? Paranoid much?"

"Dzunukwa is dead, Koi. And if what Kwaskwi suspects is true, humans killed her. Humans don't kill Kind."

"Mangasar Hayk," I said, striding forward to turn the corner onto NW Thurman. The professor who'd been ridden by the dragon-spirit Ullikemi had channeled Kind power. But he'd been utterly and helplessly human in the end.

"An exception."

I said nothing more, choosing to zero in on festive French flags displayed proudly over black awnings. A row of glass and metal bistro tables marked the outside of St. Honore. Inside was the usual crowd, and Ken turned on his friendly salesman look again as he slid close behind me in line. I surveyed the pastries, quiches, and baguette sandwiches that, on any other day, would cause me to salivate. Today, though, even the signature Choux Puff with vanilla bean custard seemed listless and sad, and my stomach clenched at the thought of eating. In my mind, the icy blue of Dzunukwa's empty eyes hovered over the blood-painted, taunting Shakespeare phrase her murderers had left like a calling card. Ken was right, there was danger here.

I pointed blindly at the first two things in the case for the slim, pony-tailed French girl at the cash register and stammered my order for a latte. Ken chose a pressed Caprese sandwich, and while we waited for the girl to box up our order his gaze settled on my hands.

"What?"

"It's the first time I've ever seen you hold a latte and not drink it."

"Not feeling thirsty I guess." I pulled out my cell phone, expecting to see a message from Marlin. It had been a couple hours but still nothing. What was she doing in her apartment for this long? *Scratch that mental image.* I didn't want to know. I juggled the latte so I could use my right hand to cancel our Kennedy School reservation.

"Is there another hotel you can suggest?" Ken asked.

"I have no idea."

Ken steered me over to an inside bistro table. "Let's sit for two minutes. I'll find us a place to stay." He broke off a piece of Caprese, gooey with melted mozzarella and pesto, and put it on a napkin in front of me. "Eat."

I put the phone down and cradled the latte in both hands, willing the warmth to seep through the paper cup into my chest to melt the frozen dread keeping me at zombie-level functionality. Automatically I held the cup to my lips and creamy bitterness slid down my throat. I gave a little groan.

Ken had switched his SIM card when we landed at PDX so he could use basic internet, and he scrolled through a Japanese travel site without getting any Caprese oil on his phone at all. An adorable pucker of concentration appeared between his eyebrows.

I decided to text Marlin. *We're going to a hotel.*

Instantly, the ellipses signifying the other person was typing a response appeared. *Where?*

I blinked. Talk about terse. She must have been madder than I thought. *I don't know yet.*

The answer came back again in a nanosecond. *Text me your location.*

A giant question mark would have appeared over my head if this were a manga. This was so unlike Marlin in tone and glaring lack of emojis. She never missed a chance to randomly insert Asian Santa, and she definitely would have used the poop emoji if she were mad.

Sorry, I typed. *Ken's being paranoid. No ginger on the hotel.*

This time the pause was longer. *No ginger?*

I stared at the phone, latte cup held forgotten to my lips. The phrase *no ginger* was a Pierce-Herai inside joke, one of those bilinguals-only phrases Marlin and I used as private sister-speak. The word *shoga* in Japanese meant ginger, but it was a homophone for *there's nothing that can be done* or *you're shit out of luck*. Marlin and I used *no ginger* whenever we wanted to be cutesy.

Whoever was texting me had Marlin's phone but it wasn't my sister. There was only one other person in her apartment when I saw her last, and he wasn't dressed to leave. Why was Pete the boy toy catfishing me? And why was he so desperate to know our hotel?

"I got us a reservation," said Ken, standing up. "Shall we go?"

"Something's wrong with Marlin. I just got the weirdest text."

"Is she okay?"

"I don't know."

"I really don't want to stay here any longer. We're still too close to Kwaskwi's men and the site where Dzunukwa was killed."

I looked at Ken and dialed my sister. It rang three times.

"*Moshi moshi.*"

At the sound of her usual greeting, tension drained from my shoulders. She was alive and close to her phone. *Way to be overly paranoid.*

"Is everything okay?"

Marlin clucked her tongue. "You're home for one day and already you dumped Dad?"

"Nurse Jenny texted you."

Ken used his manly hand-on-my-elbow-sleeve technique to steer us through the burgeoning crowd of hipsters in beanies and button-down polka dot blouses nibbling butter pastry. We emerged into bright, cold sunlight.

"She said he's non-responsive."

"Why do you think I texted you so much? I was trying to explain. You're the one who shut the door on that conversation."

"You showed up at my apartment at nine in the morning! I had company."

"I saw. How well do you know Thor?"

"Who?"

"Uh, Pete?"

"That is not a conversation you get to have with me, Ms. Magical Mysterious Foxman lover."

"Ken is not a fox."

Marlin gave a disbelieving scoff. "The point I'm making here is that you dragged Dad to Japan with promises that things were going to get better. You left me all alone."

There was no definition of alone that accounted for Marlin's pubbing posse, her extensive network of interior decorating clients, and high school friends, but her voice sounded tight and husky. Before last year when I got serious about my accounting degree and stepped up for my share of Dad's care, I was the one who relied on Marlin. Outwardly, she had it all together—a condo and a career at the age of twenty-two. I was the black sheep, the one barely scraping by with rent. Now we were redefining our roles as sisters and it wasn't comfortable for either of us.

"Things will be better," I said, considering how much I could tell her about Dad's condition and why I was back from Japan so early. My urge to protect her from the world of the Kind warred with my deep desire to share this with my wise little sister. But walking down NW Thurman while Ken hailed us a taxi wasn't the time nor place for this conversation.

"I'll go see Dad. Does he need a doctor?"

"He's going to need an IV," I said. "But doctors won't be able to fix what's wrong with him."

There was a heavy pause. "This is Baku stuff, right?"

"Yeah. He kind of over-extended himself. Pon-suma says he could wake up anytime."

"And who's that?"

"He was with us this morning."

"Yes, right. Okay, well, when are you going to come over?"

I didn't want Marlin mixed up with this Dzunukwa business. But I also planned on telling her about it. Not telling her about dangerous things had backfired before, when Mangasar Hayk threatened her to control me. I swore I wasn't going to repeat Dad's mistakes with Marlin. "Maybe tonight? If not, then definitely tomorrow morning. You have clients?"

"Naw, staying in tonight with Pete. He's getting Pad Thai and I'm introducing him to Akira Kurosawa movies."

Pete must be a big deal if she was already forcing Dad movies on him. "Tell me please not *Ran*, the battle scenes are so long and boring."

"Pete likes action. I thought I'd ease him in with *Seven Samurai*."

We ended the call with the usual things we always said, but there was a scratchy tightness in my throat, as if there were things I should have told her or things I should have made her tell me.

CHAPTER SIX

Ken gave the directions to the taxi while I used my phone to look up the Shakespeare quote, Portland Neo-Nazis and Uffheim. There were tons of information about white supremacists on the Southern Poverty Law Center website, including a disturbing hate map. But I couldn't find anything specifically PDX-related for the Nordvast Uffheim. When I glanced up, the taxi was pulling to the curb in front of the Heathman Hotel's stone façade smack dab in the middle of downtown.

"Are you kidding me? How deep is this Beefeater obsession?"

Ken paid the taxi driver with a credit card, jumped out, and took a selfie with the red-liveried doorman, who stuck his black, flower-brimmed hat on Ken's head. *Too damn adorable.*

"Tell me that you didn't choose this hotel just for a selfie that you can't even post!" It felt disloyal to Kwaskwi to be playful under the warm morning sun.

Ken grinned like a boy. It was the first time since Aomori I'd seen him anything but morose, disapproving, or confused. It called to mind what drew me to him in the first place and it was hard not to smile back, but I marshaled a stern expression. "There's no way I can afford this."

Ken held up a Platinum American Express card. "The Council hasn't cancelled my business card yet."

"In that case, lead on!"

Ken put out his arm like we were entering a ballroom. I slipped my arm through his and shouldered my bag on the other side. We crowded together into the same slot of the revolving door. Ken rested his hands lightly on my waist from behind as we shuffled through. The warmth of his strong fingers and large palms seeped through my clothing. My body took it as a signal to release my last vestige of strength. Exhaustion washed over me. I needed a bed. Soon.

I slumped on the royal blue round settee in the middle of the lobby while Ken went to the front desk. It was a small stand emblazoned with a gold rising sun. There was a huge gold mural behind it with a peacock and crane in the style of Japanese painted screens. I'd seen similar images in the memory dream fragments Ken gave me of Tokyo Council meetings hundreds of years ago. In my jet lagged fugue, it felt like I had carried those fragments with me all the way from Japan. The memories of the old Council and their traditional ways deepened this newly forged connection to Dad's country. But what we had done in Tokyo to defy that Council was a seismic shift in Tokyo Kind politics that was shaking up Kind communities all over the Pacific Basin, or so Ken informed me. Murase, Midori, Ken's sister Ben—all of Ken's family had become startlingly important to me in the short week I'd spent in Japan. They crowded into my small circle of intimates that since Mom died, included mostly Marlin and Dad.

After a few minutes, Ken came over and extended a hand. I grasped his sleeved wrist. He looked down, eyebrows bunching together and pulled me to a standing position.

"What?"

"It just struck me," said Ken in English, despite not needing to include Elise in the conversation anymore. Apparently speaking English went along with Anglophile hotels. "You could wear gloves."

I scoffed in the back of my throat. "You don't understand the basic concept of denial. Yeah, that worked well in the winter but I'm a jeans and sweatshirt kind of girl. Imagine me trying to pull off debutante or retro chic in the summer? People stared. And I was constantly having to scrub coffee stains off the gloves. I was already a freak. I preferred to be a freak under the radar."

"Ah," said Ken. "Then you've had to be very careful in public." I could see his mind follow that lonely path to its logical conclusion. But he stopped himself from pursuing the subject further. I didn't need or want his sympathy. I wasn't that Koi anymore.

Inside the elevator Ken took my bag and slung it over his shoulder. He reached across and tucked a stray piece of hair behind my ear. I shivered at the ambient warmth of his fingers near the sensitive skin. He held my gaze for a moment, not demanding, but questioning. The hotel must have had the heater cranked to full blast in the elevator because a hot flush crept across my scalp and then spread down my neck to my shoulders.

"I don't want to be a freak," I said.

"I know."

"Kwaskwi is really angry I wouldn't force a fragment from that guy. What if," my voice broke into a husky rasp, "he was one of those Nordvast Uffheim? What if he helped do that to Dzunukwa?"

The elevator dinged, and the door slid open. "Brian didn't seem capable of the violence done to her. At the most, he was a wannabe." Ken led the way down the wood-paneled hall, stopping in front of a door titled Warhol Suite.

How big was his expense account? Yikes.

Ken opened the door to the most extravagant room I'd ever stepped foot in. There was a crazy luxurious shag carpet, a purple velvet couch, and a Warhol print of Marilyn Monroe above the king-sized bed. I pinned Ken with a glare. "One bed?"

"I didn't think you'd want to be alone."

I sighed. He was probably right. But it wouldn't do to let him know that. I beelined for the bathroom, eager to discover the rich delights of shampoo and lotions of this high-end hotel.

When I emerged in one of Ken's t-shirts and booty shorts, hair damp, smelling of body lotion that likely cost the same as my rent, Ken was texting on the bed in a red pair of drawstring flannel pants with tiny penguins. And nothing else. It should have been cutesy, but I was too busy looking at his smooth, bare chest, and the long, swimmer-lithe muscles of his forearms. My hands curled at my sides, my palms remembering the texture and heat of his skin.

Bring it down a notch. I am too raw for this. No way were we navigating through the hot mess of what Ken and I were to each other right now. Chill pill time. Ken looked up and patted the bed next to him. "I'm going to brush my teeth if you're done in there? I was just letting Ben know about Dzunukwa."

He was texting his sister out in the open now? For a long time while Ken was playing Council assassin he'd pretended to be estranged from his family. "How are things in Tokyo? Did Tojo settle down? Or is he still on a rampage?"

Ken switched to Japanese, as if talking about Japan wasn't done in English. "Ben-chan says Kawano-sama and Tomoe-chan have him under control." A quiet hush deepened Ken's voice. "Things might really be changing on the Council."

I checked my phone to make sure there was nothing from Nurse Jenny or Marlin. There wasn't. The curious lack of messages or emails made me pouty. I crawled under the thousand thread Egyptian cotton sheets and turned on my side. Maybe I could fall asleep while Ken was in the bathroom and forego any awkward maneuvering in bed. I closed my eyes.

The next thing I knew the clock told me it was three hours later. Early evening setting sun filtered past the purple satin drapes, darkening the green walls into kaffir lime. I'd slept too long. Groggy from wakening from middle-of-the-night depth of sleep, I pushed the covers aside and sat up. My tongue was dry and swollen. My mouth tasted of ass. A tightening acid sting in my stomach reminded me that I hadn't taken advantage of St. Honore. I scanned the room. Someone misplaced the to-go bag.

Can the Council's credit card handle a bit of room service?

Ken was curled up on his side. The man didn't snore, and despite being deeply asleep, didn't even mouth breathe. I leaned in, taking in his musky scent, relishing the chance to gaze at the way his hair, now mousse-less, curled over his neck in a vulnerable way. I rolled off the tall bed.

Back to paradise, a.k.a. the marble bathroom, to brush my teeth and run a damp brush through my hair so it settled into a ponytail at the nape of my neck. There was a handy menu by the phone. The lobster ravioli with vanilla beurre blanc sauce was tempting, but my body clamored for breakfast. I dialed room service after slipping the Platinum card from the wallet clip stashed in Ken's carefully folded pants and ordered an omelet of spinach, mushroom and chevre. As an afterthought I added corned beef hash with poached eggs for Ken.

I picked up my phone to call Marlin, but there were phone and text notifications filling up my screen from Kwaskwi and Pon-suma.

There had been another attack. This time it was Elise.

CHAPTER SEVEN

I had to literally roll Ken out of the bed to get him awake. He hit the floor with a satisfying thunk and then blinked up at me with a wounded expression. He leaned against the bed, scratching his head roughly with both hands as I played Pon-suma's succinct voicemail message on the speaker.

Elise was attacked after driving home from McLeay Park. Two men had jumped her on the street outside her house near Mt. Tabor. Kwaskwi had taken the precaution of sending a couple of jays to follow her home. They'd run off the attackers but not before Elise had been hurt.

Kwaskwi's texts were direct. *Meet me at Elise's house. Come now or the jays will bring you.*

Ken groaned but stood up. While he went into the bathroom, I texted Marlin that I would not make it to her house tonight.

Immediately she replied with a poop emoji and a gold carp. *Checked Dad into overnight care after getting Dr. Brown to take a look. She said he has good color for someone unconscious. Tomorrow morning your ass better be here. With chocolate croissants.*

Marlin was the only person I knew as obsessed with pastry as me. That wasn't saying much considering my miniscule inner circle, but the reference to pastries and the emoji gave me a sense of relief. I'd been halfway expecting another terse, weird exchange.

Ken came out of the shower, lower half wrapped in a towel large enough to cover a family of four, just as a knock sounded. He jerked his chin at the door, going into a fight-ready mode that made the towel gape open dangerously. "Who's that?"

"Room Service!" came a voice.

"Did you order that?"

"Yeah," I said. "So stand down."

"You still don't take this seriously? That's two attacks in two days."

"I'm taking this seriously. I'm getting dressed."

Ken rolled his eyes. I went to the door and opened it to the youngest, prettiest platinum blonde bellhop I'd ever seen. She pushed a trolley into the room laden with two fine china plates covered with silver domes. The entire process of transferring the plates to the small table was mysteriously accomplished without taking her eyes from Ken, who loomed in the corner with his arms crossed and damp hair falling over his left eye. When she left, she gave a significant smile to Ken and a bland nod to me.

"Oh darn," I said in an exaggerated way. "I totally forgot to tip the hussy, I mean bellhop."

Ken fluttered his eyelashes, glancing at me from under the thick fringe in a flirtatious glance as skillful as any Southern Belle.

"We don't have time for that."

"We don't have time for," Ken came over to the table and picked up a silver dome, "corned beef hash and omelet."

"I didn't know that when I ordered." I grabbed a fork and shoved a mouthful of perfectly seasoned and browned potatoes into my mouth. I continued stealing bites while pulling on the one clean t-shirt I'd packed in my carryon bag and the loose black cotton yoga pants from the plane. Wrinkling my nose at the funky smell, I promised myself I'd hit Target to get another pair soon. Ken offered me one of his hoodies against the chill.

Within ten minutes we were both dressed and half the omelet was gone. Ken put the silver dome over the corned beef hash and called the concierge to reserve a taxi. Outside the hotel, the doorman gave Ken a three fingered salute and ushered us into a waiting Rose City Taxi driven by a young dude in a turban sporting facial hair that had never seen a razor or grooming product. I explained the address, and we were off.

Ken scrolled through his messages. "Pon-suma says Elise needs stitches and her arm is dislocated."

I winced. "She's alive, though."

"Yes. And she got a glimpse of her attackers."

I switched to Japanese with a glance at the driver. He didn't look like he was listening, but contrary to what Ken believed, I *was* feeling cautious. "Why does Kwaskwi want us there? We're not detectives."

Ken tapped his nose. "You're not the only one with helpful capabilities."

I remembered how Ken had once tracked Dad from my apartment to a bus stop by smell alone. That seemed like a million years ago, and since then I'd seen some of Ken's other helpful capabilities, including taking down three Council guards single-handedly. "Let me rephrase, why does he want *me* there?"

Ken cocked his head at an angle. "For protection, to reassure Elise, to make a statement of strength for the Portland Kind community, because Kwaskwi considers you a friend—but none of these things are really sinking into your thick brain, are they?"

I met his gaze with a set jaw. "Don't patronize me."

Ken gave an exasperated hiss. "It's literally not possible for me to patronize you. You're the most powerful Kind besides Thunderbird in Portland right now. But you do an ill turn to the Siwash Tyee and yourself by acting as if you haven't fought Mangasar Hayk and Tojo, the butcher of Nanking, and lived to tell about it."

My jaw dropped. The nerve. Who was he to get off berating me for not fully inhabiting my Kind self? He was the poster boy for constantly second-guessing himself as the assassin Bringer. And who punished themselves for years by estranging himself from everyone in his family except Ben, and pretending to be a Council slave? *It's not just me fooling myself emo fox.*

I did see Ken's point about my powers, though. Not that I'd admit it to him. Kwaskwi needed powerful allies since he couldn't just saunter up to a police station. "What's it to you anyway?"

"That's the question, isn't it?" Ken wasn't backing down. We stared at each other, a yearning ache in his eyes and frustration in mine. Then he arched an eyebrow, breaking the tension. "You are...your father and you," he swallowed down whatever he was trying to say with a raw jerk of his Adam's apple. "I keep returning to you, like a bright beacon."

The taxi pulled to a stop. I broke away from Ken to find we'd arrived in front of a red bungalow two houses away from the staircase and ramp that wound their way to the top of Mt. Tabor's extinct cinder cone. Towering rows of Douglas Fir and Norway Spruce made the air a noticeable few degrees chillier and thickened the waxing twilight. As Ken paid the taxi driver, I got out.

There wasn't a soul in sight. No moms with strollers in active wear and headbands, no bushy-bearded bike fanatics or kids aiming for the awesome playground at the top. Not even dog walkers. Just a familiar green Subaru parked across the street. The doors opened, and Henry and George extracted their burly bodies and crossed over to greet us.

"Oh gosh this is terrible. I can't believe they hurt poor Elise. I mean, she's not like Dzunukwa, frosty and mean all the time, threatening to freeze the lungs from your body, I mean, Elise can be cranky too if she doesn't get her way, but who would target her? She's Hafu but doesn't show any of her Kobold mother's characteristics so

46

she isn't scary, I mean, geez, her house is always a mess—"

George cut off the rest of Henry's rambling monologue by punching him on the shoulder. "Hey!" Henry's lower lip poofed out. "Okay, okay. George says I'm supposed to bring you around the back of the house."

I didn't see George's mouth move at all, but Ken nodded. We followed Henry up a slight incline of overgrown grass and clumps of scraggly butterfly bushes bordered by broken and sliding pieces of river shale. I sifted through the info bomb Henry had just dropped. Elise was a Kobold? Was that from Germany? One of the most famous settlers in this area, John Jakob Astor of cute coastal town Astoria fame was German, so that kind of made sense. I thought Kobolds were like miners or cave elves, though, not annoying blonde cheerleader-types.

And Elise was Hafu, like me. Like Ken. I'd figured out that Hafu were on a continuum in terms of their Kind attributes. I had inherited almost all of Dad's Baku-ness, or at least we hadn't tested the limits yet. Ken and his sister Ben definitely had Kitsune illusion powers but they were nothing compared to Tojo—a full Kitsune— who I'd seen set Ben on fire with his illusion. I'd felt the heat of the flames myself.

Ken's stepmother, Midori, was also Hafu, I gathered, but manifested nothing at all of her Kitsune background. Maybe Elise was like Midori. But instead of nursing everyone, she acted as a spy and gofer. Kwaskwi had sent Elise to spy on me through joining my PCC classes back before I even knew I was Baku, or any of this craziness had started. At some point I'd have to get over my resentment of her.

Now would be an excellent time considering the attack.

The bungalow's roof sported a row of blue jays, a sure sign their master was in attendance. I looked down at the concrete patio.

"Had your beauty sleep?" Kwaskwi sat on a fire-engine red Adirondack chair, his leather riding boots propped on top of an overly large ceramic garden gnome statue dressed in a stocking cap. Pon-suma was nowhere in sight.

"I'm sorry, Kwaskwi. How is she doing?"

"Cut the bullshit, Koi." He stood up. "This is on you."

The skin on my face stung like he'd physically slapped me. "Even if I'd forced a fragment from that Brian guy, there is no guarantee he saw anything more useful than the Skin Head group he already gave us."

"They knocked her unconscious. One of them sliced up her back."

"That's sick."

"Come on, then."

"Where are we going?"

Kwaskwi crossed his arms, standing silently while the jays above him jittered and scolded and squawked.

"There's no guarantee she saw anything useful! Or that she's dreaming about it!"

"You can't argue this time. Elise is Kind. She knows what you're capable of. She would have given her consent." He nodded at the Bear Brothers. They flanked me. Henry's genial smile faded away.

"Koi is of more use when she is willing," Ken said.

I held up my hands, palms out. "Okay, okay. No need for George and Henry to get jiggy with me," I said, aiming a frown at Henry. He cleared his throat and bent down to retie his size twenty sneakers. George gave a barely perceptible wince. "I'll try to get a fragment from Elise. Show me."

Kwaskwi released a long, slow breath. "This way." He leaped up the back steps and held the screen door open for me. We passed through a canary yellow tiled kitchen, a hallway lined with photos of Elise with other blondes of various ages I guessed were family, and into the living room. It was all dark wood beams and casement windows. Elise lay on a beige couch studded with turquoise and emerald velveteen pillows. She was face down, her head turned to the side. A white sheet draped her from the neck down. Next to her knelt a young man with porcelain skin, curly blonde hair which hung down below his ears, and an aquiline nose that looked more unsure of itself than patrician. He was dressed in scrubs and had a stethoscope around his neck.

"She's still unconscious," he said.

"This is Koi," said Kwaskwi. He nodded at the man. "Chet is Elise's cousin. He's studying to be a physician's assistant at OHSU."

Chet stood up. He was about the same height as me, despite giving off a taller, more angular impression. I wondered if he was a human or Kobold side cousin. "You're the Baku." He stuck out a hand. "Nice to meet you."

This was such a normal, human reaction that I simply stared at him, eyes wide. Kwaskwi saw my consternation and guffawed. "You handle Thunderbird and the Bears, but Chet Muehler makes you speechless?" He elbowed Ken, who had padded up behind me. "You're going to have to step up your game now that she's meeting other presentable Kind. You've lost your advantage."

"I don't shake hands," I said. Kwaskwi in this mood was annoying. But I was grateful to have the joker back instead of the stern accuser.

"Of course," said Chet, wiping his palms on his thighs. "Pardon me." He retreated to the couch. Tendrils of Elise's messy ponytail fluttered with her breath. She looked extremely vulnerable lying there. "Take a look at this." He turned back the sheet.

Someone had indeed sliced up Elise's back. Porcelain skin must have been a familial trait. It was a perfect contrast for the deep, red cuts. Henry gasped, hiding his face in the crook of his elbow. George led him towards the front door.

Kwaskwi approached. "That's a pattern."

"Yes," said Chet. "Geometrical triangles. I've never seen anything like it. I don't think it's Kind."

"I've seen it," said Ken. "In Koi's apartment."

I forced myself to look at Elise's violated skin, swallowing down the acid-potato taste surging in the back of my throat. Ken was right. It was three interlocking triangles. The backs of my knees met the glass coffee table before I even realized I was in retreat. I sat down heavily on top of a photograph essay book on Portland coffee houses that was the same edition I'd given Marlin for Christmas last year. "No," I said. More proof. Whoever trashed my apartment was the same person who attacked Elise. The same person who killed Dzunukwa.

Ken explained the details of the quote and symbols left in my apartment to everyone.

"That's the other half of the quote from the Witch's Castle. *From this sleep of death, what dreams may come.* It's calling out a Baku. Why else mention dreams?" Kwaskwi rounded on me, anger sparking off him. "You can't hide from this anymore, Koi. No more lying."

The front door banged opened and Pon-suma came in. His hands were grimy with dirt, his unbound hair tangled with bits of leaves and twigs, and he wore only shorts. Chet gave an appraising glance over Pon-suma's slim, hairless chest as he reached over to settle the sheet around Elise's shoulders again. The Horkew Kamuy spoke to Kwaskwi. "Human. No trace of anything else."

"Then the jays are right." Kwaskwi shoved me in the back. "You're up. Get an image of who did this. All I need is a description. We'll find the bastards."

"There's more," Pon-suma interrupted. "A phrase in pig's blood on the sidewalk."

My chest tightened. *Please, oh please don't let it be another dream reference.*

"What does it say?" Kwaskwi demanded.

"The whole world is a dream, and death is the interpreter."

CHAPTER EIGHT

Kwaskwi gripped my hoodie's drawstrings and jerked me up, half-choking. "What did you do, Koi? How did you piss off Neo-Nazis?"

Ken gave a quiet cough, standing very close. Kwaskwi let me go with a loud kiss against his teeth. I shuddered, breathing too fast. My heart beat a rapid tattoo inside my ribs. I inched backwards until I felt the bolstering warmth of Ken's chest.

"Neo-Nazis?" Chet repeated.

Ken held out his phone, flashing a pic from the Southern Poverty Law Center site of an angry, unwashed white guy proudly displaying a chest tattoo of three interlocking triangles. "This is a Portland picture. You can see Mt. Hood in the background."

"Why are Neo-Nazis quoting Shakespeare at Koi?"

Ken shook his head. "I'm not convinced this is directed at Koi."

Kwaskwi snorted. "I'm not convinced you see clearly through your desperate need for forgiveness."

I gestured at Elise. "You've had her spying on me for god knows how long. I go to PCC classes. I go to Marlin's condo. As far as I know Stumptown isn't a hive of white supremacist activity. Since things started to go crazy you've literally been with me the whole time. When would I have time to piss off Nazis?"

"Akihito," said Kwaskwi.

"My father's been in adult day care or in a coma. Unless Neo-Nazis are suddenly volunteering at Salvation Army, I don't see how he could be mixed up in this."

"Your father has had a long life. There is much you don't know about him." Point for Kwaskwi. Revelations about who Dad was before meeting Mom, opening Marinopolis, and fathering two girls were a little hole in the fabric of my heart, and I ignored the unraveling edges for fear of what I might find. When I looked back on my childhood, of what I thought he was, of who I thought I was, there was no way to tell what was true and what was the result of Dad hiding.

"White supremacists are human," said Ken. "With human lifespans. These attacks couldn't be a result of grudges from Herai-san's prior life."

"Attackers were human. They had Kind helpers?" said Pon-suma.

Kwaskwi made a shooing motion with his hands at Chet and Pon-suma. They sidled out of the way. "Conjecture wastes time. Do your thing, Baby Baku."

I took a deep breath. Kwaskwi was right, Elise knew what I was. She would want to help in any way possible to stop these attacks. Still, what I was about to do felt like a grave invasion of privacy. Not to mention I was not looking forward to experiencing life a la cheerleader spy.

I glanced up at Ken. His eyebrows were knit together over eyes dark with concern. He gave a little nod, reassuring me he was there to pull me out if something went haywire. Although, what could go wrong? The dreams and memory fragments of ancient Kind like Ullikemi, the Black Pearl, and Thunderbird were powerful vortexes that drew me in and threatened to overwhelm the small Koi-self flame that sustained me when I dreamed other people's dreams. But

Elise wasn't even full Kind. She was more human that I was. Human dreams that used to invade my sleep as a young girl, making it impossible to keep stranger's worries and desires from my own, were nothing now. Cobwebs to be brushed away.

So get on with it.

I went over to the sofa and knelt on the floor next to Elise. She was so very pale. Part of my hesitation was that Dad wasn't the only person experiencing dream eating blowback. My sight had returned in the airplane, but I'd burned myself to a cinder releasing the Black Pearl back in Aomori. I half hoped I was still burned out, but when I rested a palm on Elise's feverish hot cheek, the room went tilt-a-whirl and for a stomach-wrenching moment, all I could do was kneel, muscles and tendons spasming out of control. Static crawled across my vision, eating away the sofa, Elise's face, and all awareness of anger and fear radiating from the four men crowded into the room. Then there was nothing but the static.

It dissipated slowly, leaching away until I was in a gray room, looking at a gray table and concrete floor. A ratchet sound, as if someone turned the dial on a padlock came from my right. A man wearing a dark hood pulled down low over his forehead entered the room. Anticipation shot through me. My lips curved into a smile. This was going exactly as I planned. The man reached to pull his hoodie down, a flash of vivid tattoo at his exposed wrist. I stopped him with a shout. "No. I can't see your face."

The flame of myself flared to life. Not me. This was not Koi. This was Elise's dream. It held the solid weight of a memory-dream, but something was off. Despite the ease separating myself from Elise within the dream, I felt disturbingly out of control and dizzy.

"Where?" said the man.

And the world went tilt-a-whirl again. When it spun itself right side up, I was in a gray room, looking at a gray table and concrete floor. A ratchet sound came from my right.

This wasn't right. *The dream is replaying!* My Koi-flame flared. I

53

was so dizzy, so confused. I would eat this dream and burn through the confusion. I let the hunger flare along with the mental image of the Koi candle-flame. The weird gray dream grew brilliant with a white light, and then began to singe black at the edges. The taste of Elise's dream was greasy and heavy, like cramming a handful of fast food fries still dripping with oil into my mouth all at once, but even that spurred the Baku hunger. I wanted more, more, and I drew eagerly at the dream.

"Stop!"

Something constricted my throat, my real throat in real life. Gasping, I blinked rapidly as Elise's dream abruptly ruptured. I was back in the living room, gripped around the throat by Kwaskwi's hand wrapped in a sheet corner. My lungs screamed for air. Ken grabbed Kwaskwi's pinky and bent it back. Kwaskwi dropped me like a sack of potatoes, and I crumpled to a heap on the floor, every muscle sore as if I'd been pounded by a meat tenderizer. *What is wrong with me? A simple fragment shouldn't hit me like this.*

"Don't do that again," Ken was saying to Kwaskwi. The two faced off at the head of the sofa, leaning forward on the balls of their feet, hands clenched into fists.

"She was hurting Elise."

"I'm glad he stopped me," I said, my voice coming out in a husky rasp. "Something was weird."

They ignored me. Testosterone and dominance crackled like ozone. Ken's features sharpened. Outside the house, the screams of jays pierced the air. Violence was imminent.

"Don't ever touch her like that again," said Ken in a quiet voice.

Chet made a small movement toward the two, but Pon-suma's hand shot out and pulled him back. The front door slammed open. George and Henry squeezed through, lumbering over to join the anger ball man-fest on Kwaskwi's side. Henry growled, like an actual animal growl. George just hunkered down, glowering under eyebrow ridges as heavy as a Neanderthal's. A prickling fizzy sensation filled the air, like the second after twisting open the cap on a shaken bottle of soda about to explode.

Elise groaned. Instantly, Chet was by her side. He took her wrist's pulse. Kwaskwi's upper lip curled into a parting sneer, and then he moved to help Chet raise Elise to a sitting position, making sure the sheet wrapped tightly around her front. Pon-suma settled in by my side, giving my shoulder a squeeze. He was itching to look me over. I had my own personal medical attendant, too. *Okay, way to be weird and petty.*

"What the fucking hell hit me?" Elise said. She fluttered her eyelashes open and groaned again. And why am I in a sheet on the couch?"

"You were attacked," Kwaskwi said.

"No shit. And then you decided to hold a jamboree in my living room?"

Chet put a cut-glass whiskey tumbler of water in her hand. "Can you drink this?'

Elise gave a gagging cough. "Anything for you, loverboy." She sipped the water, and then promptly began another round of hacking and coughing. "Why does my mouth taste like ash?" Her eyes widened, going from unfocused to zeroing in on me. "And what the hell is the Baku doing in my house?"

"I need information, Elise," said Kwaskwi.

George and Henry stood down, lounging on bookend easy chairs on either side of the sofa. Kwaskwi sat carefully next to Elise, holding her hand in a gentle, reassuring way that I envied with all my heart. If only Ken or Pon-suma would hold my hand. I needed reassurance, too. The feeling of Elise's strange repeat-dream still hung like a miasma of greasy smoke in my brain. Worse, the Baku hunger had spurred me across the line in the sand I'd drawn between Koi Pierce and Koi the Monster. Maybe it had something to do with trying to dream eat after being burned out. I wasn't sure.

"You let her poke around in my brain?"

"I asked her to," said Kwaskwi. He glowered in my direction. "Although I didn't ask her to start eating your very soul from your body."

"Hey. That's not fair," I protested.

"Did you get anything worthwhile?" asked Elise, oddly curious instead of horrified as I'd expected. She leaned forward, eager.

I shook my head. "The dream that I was eating was just a gray room and a man. I don't even think it was a true memory dream. It definitely didn't have anything to do with you being attacked."

Kwaskwi straightened, letting Elise's hand drop. "What man?"

"It wasn't an attacker. Just a guy in a hoodie with tattoos."

Elise stiffened. "A guy in a hoodie? I don't think that's who attacked me. They came at me from behind, but I don't remember hoodies."

Kwaskwi scoffed. "Well that was totally helpful." He bowed into his hands, resting his elbows on his knees. It struck me that his anger stemmed from fear for Elise and his people. All of a sudden, I wasn't just jealous of hand-holding, but of the whole package Elise enjoyed: Kwaskwi to care for her, Bear Brothers who would come running when she was in trouble, a sense that she belonged to people.

I wanted those things.

My phone buzzed. I backed away from the sofa conversation and went back into the hallway.

I'm sorry about this morning. Marlin had added a sheepish face emoji.

S'okay.

Are you eating dinner?

I'm actually with Ken and Kwaskwi.

Where?

I stared at the words for a moment, feeling uneasy with how terse Marlin was. And also, if I admitted the truth, feeling oddly hurt that she was more interested in where I was having dinner than talking about Dad or asking about my apartment or how I was doing.

Do you remember Elise?

Yes.

At her house, I typed.

How is she?

Okay, now that was a weird question for Marlin to ask. And I couldn't even remember when Elise and Marlin would have been in the same room together. I remembered the strange text conversation we'd had before felt, and how my attempt to nudge Marlin into a better mood with our shared joke of *no ginger* had bombed.

Pon-suma stuck his head into the hallway. "Kwaskwi wants you."

I nodded, relieved to have an excuse to cut this short. I'd deal with Marlin tomorrow morning and straighten out all this weirdness then.

Talk more later. I slipped the phone back into my pocket.

Back in the living room, Kwaskwi looked as if he were holding court, with Chet playing secretary with a pad of paper and a pen, Ken glowering in the corner, and Pon-suma standing in his usual military casual, implacable stance next to Ken.

"…with everyone together tonight, there will be less chance of the Nordvast Uffheim attacking anyone else," Kwaskwi was saying. He jabbed a finger in the air at me. "That means you, too, Koi. They've definitely got the hots for a dream eater. I don't want you alone out there tonight."

"She's not alone," said Ken.

Kwaskwi grimaced. "Also it will be a good chance for you to see everyone and for everyone to see you. The stories going around make you out like a cross between Xena Warrior Princess and Buffy the Vampire Slayer."

Elise laughed. "Ha. More like Willow. When her sweaters were nerdy before she became Wiccan."

Elise is definitely not a fan. But can I blame her? I entered her dreams when she was unconscious. Not what you would expect from a BFF.

"See me where?" I decided to stand next to Pon-suma as a

statement of neutrality. Ken's feral Kitsune was showing, making him cranky faced.

Henry was a pot that bubbled over at my question. I could just see how the effort to remain silent had twisted him in knots. "At the bonfire! We'll gather at Broughton Bluffs all together. You know, along the Sandy River? The entrance is by Lewis & Clark Recreation area. We'll have a giant bonfire and say our final goodbyes to Dzunukwa. Like a Viking sendoff only on land. It's usually potluck, but Kwaskwi said since its short notice he'll order catering. I'm hoping for Podnah's BBQ 'cause mmmmm, love that salt-crusted brisket, but for dessert we can definitely roast marshmallows, better not forget the Hershey's." He took a breath and saw the shocked expression of distaste on my face. "Not on Dzunukwa's bonfire, of course not, she's Kwakwaka'wakw like us, right? We will be respectful. There'll be lots of little fires, too and someone always brings hard cider and beer. Do you drink? It's okay if you don't. There's plenty that don't. George doesn't drink. He says I drink enough for the both of us."

George made a little chopping gesture and Henry clammed up like someone had pulled his electrical plug. I stifled a laugh. The quiet Bear Brother gave a dry cough.

"George says we should get going. Lots of people to see," said Henry. The Bear Brothers stood. "See you at the cremation."

CHAPTER NINE

Kwaskwi and Chet were preoccupied with Elise and it became clear after an awkward moment that Elise wished I would leave. I didn't know this neighborhood as well as Southwest, but it was Portland. There either had to be a microbrewery or a coffee shop within a few blocks.

"Can we get some air?" I asked Ken.

He looked at Kwaskwi, who paused in dictating to Chet a list of bonfire supplies and made a dismissive gesture with his hand. "Don't go far. It could still be dangerous."

Pon-suma cleared his throat. "I'll come, too."

Kwaskwi didn't pause this time. I felt a twinge of sympathy. Pon-suma came to Portland at Kwaskwi's request but was clearly out of his element. Kwaskwi was caught up with Elise and a young, muscled hottie that clearly had a shared past with the other two. Their intimacy placed Pon-suma squarely on the outside.

"Kwaskwi's right, you know," said Ken in Japanese as we went down the front steps. He waited while I scanned both directions. To the right, it looked like residential streets. My coffee-dar was beeping more to the left.

"Let's go this way." The boys filed after me.

"About what?" I threw over my shoulder.

"Those quotations are aimed at you. Or Herai-san."

I stopped abruptly. "I don't see how that can be possible. I mean, I just found out myself a few weeks ago about the existence of Baku."

Pon-suma and Ken exchanged a charged glance. "Do you think I'm next on the attack list?"

Ken shook his head. "I don't know. If it is humans, they are exhibiting canny behavior. Picking off Kind one by one. First a loner like Dzunukwa. Then a weaker Kind like Elise. But I don't see how that has anything to do with you, Koi, unless they think it's you and not Kwaskwi who is in charge."

"The second quotation?" Pon-suma said.

I pulled out my phone again and Googled it. "There's no official attribution. It's supposedly a Yiddish proverb. *The whole world is a dream, and death is the interpreter.*"

"Both quotations mention dreams and death," said Ken.

"Yeah, I noticed. They're using death as a taunt. Even powerful Kind like Baku are powerless in the face of mortality."

Ken gave me an appraising look.

"What? I read. I think about things. What else would introverts do besides ponder weighty philosophical matters?"

"Binge-watch Netflix and scarf Ben & Jerry's," said Ken, arching an eyebrow.

Pon-suma looked confused. Definitely not as up to date on Americana as Ken. I routinely underestimated Ken's pop-cultural knowledge.

I fell in next to Ken, meaning the two guys hogged the sidewalk while I traversed uneven front lawns and dodged prickly landscaping. Pon-suma huffed. "Thunderbird is the most powerful here, not Koi-chan."

"Maybe they don't know about Thunderbird," I said.

"Kwaskwi should keep it that way," said Ken. He speared Pon-suma with a serious look. "You should suggest that Thunderbird not come to the bonfire tonight."

Pon-suma looked down at the sidewalk. "Me?"

"We know for a fact he won't listen to me."

A commercial district came into sight. I pointed at a building with dark siding that said *Rain or Shine Café* on the window. "I'll tell him, too. Maybe that will get through that thick skull of his."

Pon-suma gave a wry grimace. I thought about Kwaskwi holding Elise's hand and decided I was going to have to put a bit of work into getting a posse of my own. I would have to disrupt a lifetime habit of shirking physical contact. *Fake it till you make it.* I linked my arm through Pon-suma's, ignoring how he stiffened in surprise. He stopped mid-stride, but I pulled him along into the shop, Ken right behind us.

As soon as I walked in, I could feel the muscles in my back relax, and the tension in my jaw melt away. This was exactly my kind of place. Sofas, benches and chairs were arranged in homey little stations where a variety of folks sat talking or staring intently into their laptops. The menu featured both Cardamom and Lavender lattes. I ordered the Cardamom and a fat croissant with a stripe of chocolate glaze.

Pon-suma and Ken got their black coffees right away and went to sit while I waited at the bar for my latte. The barista was a guy about my age wearing a beanie and sporting a full sleeve black tribal tattoo featuring a repeated pattern like scales and an angry, swirly face with a large grimacing mouth on his left arm.

"Nice ink," I said while he pulled my espresso shot.

"Thanks." He flashed a noncommittal service industry smile.

The ink on the hoodie guy in Elise's dream jiggled my memory. "It's cool to see something other than a Celtic knot."

"I know, right? I designed this myself. It's based on Maori folk art."

"Lit."

The barista formed a heart on my latte with the last of the foamed milk. His smile loosened into friendliness as he handed it over to me.

"Hey," I said. "You ever seen guys around here with sleeves that included three interlocking triangles?"

The smile dropped away. The barista held up his hands and backed away from the bar. "Hey now, I don't want any part of that. All are welcome here. This isn't Gresham."

"Ah, sorry." I grabbed my latte and hightailed it over to the boys. It had only been a hunch to ask about the tattoos but the barista had reacted so strongly it made me suspect that the Rain or Shine Café had experience with the kind of guys who hung out with Nordvast Uffheim.

They'd been around the area. They'd attacked both Elise and Dzunukwa and for some reason they were taunting me. Or Dad. Ken put down his coffee on a wooden end table. I broke off a piece of luscious croissant and shoved it into my mouth.

"Before World War II, the Kind of San Francisco were concentrated around China Town. The Shishin and the Tong made a mutual protection pact that angered the Tokyo Council," said Ken.

"Another random history lesson?"

Pon-suma put a fist to his mouth, covering a smile.

"I'm just asking because I don't have anything to take notes with."

"Very funny," said Ken in a low tone that made it clear this wasn't time for banter. "They sent me in as Bringer to break up that pact. I could have taken out Tong heads, or I could have followed the Shishin's flunkies and roughed them up."

"What are the Shishin, anyway?"

Pon-suma's smile widened to a smirk. So glad my Kind ignorance amused him. Ken shook his head, eyes closed. "They are the four divine beast guardians of the compass points; bird, dragon, turtle, tiger. They run the southwest seaboard here in the states."

"You single-handedly went after four divine beasts?"

"I went directly after the strongest force," Ken said at the same time. He blinked at me. "I think that's what the Nordvast Uffheim are doing here in Portland. Take down the strongest, most obvious leader and the rest will fall into place."

"So why the mysterious quotes, then? And why us, why not Kwaskwi? He's the obvious leader."

"The Siwash Tyee has power," said Pon-suma slowly. "He is not most powerful."

"It is unsettling that the Nordvast Uffheim didn't choose him as their target. I thought it was not apparent from the outside that Kwaskwi isn't the most powerful Kind in Portland," Ken said.

Pon-suma stood up. "Insider information."

"Yes. How else would they find Dzunukwa? Identify Elise as belonging to the Kind? Go after a Baku instead of Kwaskwi?" Ken stood up, too. He pointed out the front window. Two blue jays perched on the concrete sill outside, staring intently in our direction with their beady little eyes. "There's a traitor. And Kwaskwi is giving them a perfect target for an attack by assembling all the Portland Kind at the bonfire."

CHAPTER TEN

I scarfed the rest of the croissant and let Ken bustle me out the coffeehouse. As soon as we emerged, the jays scolded and jeered, launching into the sky and winging towards Elise's house. We double-timed it back to her bungalow. George and Henry's Subaru idled at the curb in front. Henry stuck his head out of the window. "Kwaskwi says we should take you to your hotel to get changed."

"No," said Ken abruptly. Henry's face fell.

"He means no thank you," I said. "We'll call a taxi. Nothing personal. Just it might be safer if you don't know where we are staying."

"Can we at least take you back to Kwaskwi's?" Henry asked Pon-suma. When he nodded an affirmative, Henry recovered his usual cheery expression.

Ken and I waved goodbye to Pon-suma as he got into the Subaru. We knocked on Elise's front door.

Kwaskwi answered. "Where's Pon-suma?"

"Henry and George gave him a ride to your place," I said. Kwaskwi looked over his shoulder at Chet and then back to me.

"That's good. There is much to discuss before Dzunukwa's bonfire. Is your father in a safe place tonight? Do I need to send guards for him?"

I considered. The attackers had chosen their victims carefully, waiting until they were alone. Dad was in the overnight nursing facility where Nurse Jenny worked. It was set up like a hospital floor with a nurse's station and rooms in a cluster. Staff were in and out all night. I didn't think the attackers wanted to involve that many people. Dad was probably safer than I was standing here in Elise's house. Besides, only Marlin and I knew his location. A precaution that, like Ken's insistence Kwaskwi not know we were at the Heathman, suddenly changed from ludicrous to necessary.

Unease sent a cold tendril down my shoulder. There was another person who might know: Pete. Who had interesting tattoos. "I'm not sure," I said, pulling out my phone. Kwaskwi pressed his lips together. I ignored the impatience steaming off him, swiping my way back to the Southern Poverty Law Center website. On the bottom of the page was a *symbols of hate* link.

The three interlocking triangles were there as well as the arrow cross. Scrolling down, the big black numerals of the number 14 stood out boldly on the page. It was a reference to a 14-word slogan. *We must secure the existence of our people and a future for white children.*

White supremacists called to my mind grainy, white-and-black photos of black-haired kids peering out from behind barbed wire. Mom had taken Marlin and me to the Oregon Nikkei Legacy center in middle school, despite Dad's protestations it had nothing to do with him, and forced me to spend several hours reading all the information at the Minidoka exhibit, the high desert internment camp in Idaho where many Oregonians were interned. Whenever Neo-Nazis or the KKK were on the news, it wasn't burning crosses, but internment camps that came to mind. How quickly and easily the hypocritical U.S. had vilified one ethnicity on one hand, while on the other claimed honor and glory fighting genocidal Germans.

A deep-rooted fear was growing in me that the Portland white supremacists had sidelined keeping their white daughters out of the hands of Blacks and Asians in favor of a new goal: ensuring the future of humanity and their human children against the Kind.

But the dark and moody Kwaskwi who'd met us at the Witch's Castle and throttled me in Elise's living room would not react well to my suspicions that Marlin's boyfriend had connections to white supremacists. What if he stormed over there right now? No way was I going to put Marlin in danger because of an uneasy feeling.

Ken and I could do a little rooting around before the bonfire and get Kwaskwi involved tonight if Pete seemed in any way hinky.

"Yeah." I finally answered Kwaskwi's impatient humming. "He's safe for now, though he's not attending the bonfire, obviously."

Elise stiffly made her way over. "See you tonight, then." Her hand was on the edge of the door, pushing, obviously ready for us to leave.

"Should you be up?" Kwaskwi said, shouldering the door open again.

"All I needed was my shoulder relocated and a bit of Chet's magic TLC." Elise gave a deliberate, unkind smile that didn't reach her eyes. "You know intimately how potent that is, don't you?"

Kwaskwi's eyes flickered sideways and down. He was embarrassed. Because Elise was letting on that he and Chet were at one time an item? Hopefully for Pon-suma's sake it was long past. What if it was now? *Not in any way part of my business.* Yet somehow Elise was enjoying the unease she'd stirred up.

"Do you know Broughton Bluff? Just take the signs toward Lewis and Clark Recreation area, but then go straight along the Sandy River road. There'll be a gated state park parking area, but don't pull in there. The park officially closes at 6pm so wait for Henry and George. They'll show you how to get onto the private property driveway."

I nodded, just as eager for us to leave as Elise was. Kwaskwi studied my face, his pupils growing wide inside the dark irises with intense emotion. He put a palm to his heart and poked me between the collarbones with three stiff fingers. "You owe me a debt, Baku. But there is more between us than debt. You'll see at tonight's bonfire what it could be like to fully embrace the Portland Kind."

My heart leaped at Kwaskwi's words. But the squirming tangle of worries inside my brain took up too much space to form a coherent answer. I tried for a serious, mature expression as I said goodbye, but Kwaskwi's worried frown as he closed the door probably meant I'd come off as constipated instead.

Ken had a taxi waiting by the curb as I came down the steps. It was the same Sikh dude as before. He gave me a little wave. "Back to the Heathman?"

"Yes, please," Ken answered. He sat shoved up against the side of the door, doing that thing where he stared at his fingers curled over his kneecaps like they were the most important thing in the world while being so painfully aware of my position that a feeling like a storm cloud coalesced into the backseat.

"I need to tell you—"

"Let me explain—"

We both lapsed into tense waiting. "You go," said Ken finally.

I switched to Japanese for privacy. "I think we need to meet Marlin now, before the bonfire. That man who answered her door? Pete. He had white supremacist tattoos."

Ken turned to face me with both eyebrows arched. "We left Marlin there with him all this time?"

"I didn't realize what they were until I saw similar symbols on the guy in Elise's dream."

"I thought you saw something. Why didn't you tell Kwaskwi?"

"I'm not sure. I guess first because it took me a while to process Elise's dream, it was so weird and gray and bland. Then I was worried Kwaskwi would send the Bear Brothers charging in to kidnap Marlin for safety's sake or insist on taking Dad."

Ken lowered his head, swallowing. He spoke in an even, calming tone that I resented because of what it implied. I wasn't hysterical. "I understand it is important to you to care for your family, but Kwaskwi is the Siwash Tyee. He cares for all Portland Kind, including you. Including Marlin."

Ken lumped me in with Kwaskwi's posse but I wasn't so sure Kwaskwi saw it that way yet. "I know. I'm not sure okay? What if Pete is just some dude who made unfortunate tattoo choices?"

"Trust your instincts, Koi. It's too much of a coincidence." Ken gave instructions to the taxi driver to head to Marlin's condo instead.

"What were you about to say just now?"

Ken's eyelids lowered halfway. He turned to the window, gazing at the lift towers over the Hawthorne Bridge's trusses. The pyramid top of the KOIN center building and the Wells Fargo building were starting to light up as evening deepened. "Nothing that matters more than Marlin."

CHAPTER ELEVEN

Only a couple of hours remained before we had to meet George and Henry at Broughton Bluffs. My jet-lagged time sense was so fogged up I had no idea if it was a weekday or weekend. Factoring in possible traffic, we needed at least an hour of buffer time. *Can't be late to my Portland Kind debut.*

Ken and I discussed texting Marlin we were coming but I, ultimately, decided against it. Marlin and Pete were supposed to be eating Pad Thai and watching movie samurai die one by one in bloody ways. In other words, relaxed. Better Pete didn't have time to come up with excuses or stories.

The driver pulled up to the curb. He asked Ken eagerly if he should wait, and I wondered if Ken was over tipping. Ken deferred to me.

"Ah, yeah. Can you come back in like thirty minutes?" How long would it take us to figure out if Pete was a murderous Neo-Nazi? Either way, we had to have him settled before the bonfire. I hoped Pon-suma didn't get a chance to discuss Thunderbird with Kwaskwi. The giant, ancient eagle's presence couldn't make the gathering any more of a target than it already was with the Portland Kind assembled in an outdoor, secluded place in the dark and if things turned ugly, Thunderbird would be mucho handy.

"Koi?" Ken stood with his head cocked to the side, scratching at stubble darkening his cheek. I realized I was watching the Sikh dude's taxi as if he were driving away with something precious. In a way, he was. Now I couldn't avoid confronting Marlin. Again, another inversion of our usual relationship where she nagged at me about how to live my life and I passively aggressively resisted. I wasn't even sure how to go about asking my sister if her boyfriend was a Nazi.

"Yeah, okay. Let's go up." Ken followed me up the outside staircase. As we walked the hallway to Marlin's door, a light smattering of drizzle accumulated in random damp spatters on the concrete walkway below. I hoped Kwaskwi had lighter fluid for his bonfire, or alternate cremation plans.

The door opened on my second round of knocking. I slumped against the wall, releasing a huge sigh. It was my sister's Pierce hazel eyes that peered out into the corridor instead of her potential Nazi boyfriend's. "Koi? What are you doing here?"

"Can I come in? There's something I have to talk to you about."

Marlin puffed out her cheeks and then released the air in a frustrated rush. "We just got to the part where the bandits are about to storm the village and set off all the booby traps. I thought you were coming tomorrow."

"No ginger," I said, watching Marlin's face intently for her reaction. "This is important."

Marlin reacted to the phrase with a shrug. "Fine, then. Come in."

Inside her living room Pete sat on the couch facing a new flat screen TV I'd never seen before. It was crammed into the rattan and bamboo hutch Marlin inherited from Mom. The rest of her apartment was more eggshell-cream Pottery Barn and Ethan Allen—a real life advertisement for her interior decorating business—than Polynesian but she made it work. That was one of Marlin's gifts, taking the eccentric and somehow making it fit into the mundane. She'd done the same with me growing up.

Ken positioned his lanky frame on a barstool in the kitchen. His tight jaw and narrow gaze were directed right at Pete. It was a challenge no one could miss. Pete glanced over and stiffened, withdrawing his arm from the back of the sofa.

Marlin pulled me into the kitchen and started her electric pot boiling water. "What's up with Mr. Kitsune?"

"Marlin!"

"What?" she said, tapping her French manicured nails on the Milk Oolong tea box. "*Kare wa Nihongo hanasai yo.*"

It didn't matter if Pete didn't speak Japanese. Marlin had no right to be so careless with Ken's nature. What else had she been careless about? Duh. The answer to how to delicately probe about Pete right in front of his face was the family language. I'd been around so many bilingual people in Japan I'd gotten out of the habit of having a private language. I switched over to Japanese, too.

"It's your new boyfriend. Have you seen his tattoos?"

Marlin shook her head. "I can't believe you're asking me that after this morning. I've seen every inch of that hot body."

I held a hand out to accept the Marinopolis Sushiland mug with the sailor-suit dressed mackerel mascot Marlin had rescued from Dad's restaurant when it closed. She always gave me that mug instead of her matching Wedgwood plate ware. I didn't know if it was sentimentality or my habit of chipping the rims of my cups.

"TMI, seriously," I said in English.

Pete came around to our side of the sofa and perched on the arm. "What's up, girls? Why the sudden Japanese chatter?"

Marlin stirred instant coffee into a Wedgwood mug full of hot water. She circled the breakfast bar to give it to Pete, running her hand along his shoulder. "Sister stuff, okay. Give me a minute?"

Instant coffee? *Could I dislike this guy any more?* I switched back to Japanese, but it was super awkward saying this while Marlin stood at Pete's side. I didn't know how to say white supremacist in Japanese, and Nazi in katakana sounded too much like Nazi in English. "His tattoos are the ones used by white guys who hate minorities."

Marlin went still. "What are you talking about?"

"Was your boyfriend with you this afternoon?" Ken interjected.

"No," said Marlin. "What happened? Why are you guys interrogating me like a detective show?"

"You know there are Portland Kind besides me and Dad. Someone has been cutting weak ones from the herd and attacking them. There's evidence that the people doing this are part of—" I caught myself before I uttered Nordvast Uffheim in katakana, yet another thing I couldn't risk Pete overhearing. "—a group of white men here in Portland."

Marlin let rip with a string of rolled r yakuza curses normally only Dad used. "You have so little faith in me that you come here accusing him of hurting people rather than trust my judgment?"

I shot Ken a desperate look. I was supposed to be swooping in to rescue Marlin, not making myself look like an asshole. I dug thumbs into my temples, pressing hard to relieve an uncomfortable pressure, the teasing first sallies of an oncoming migraine. "You never mentioned him before I went to Japan, I just feel like he came into your life awfully fast."

Marlin pointed a finger up at my face, coming close enough that I could smell the garlic and ginger on her breath. "*You* will not lecture *me* about my love life. I don't tell you every damn thing about who I date, Koi, because I feel sorry for *you*."

Low blow, little sister. A flash of heat rolled down from the crown of my head to redden my cheeks. Sweat dewed my armpits. Angry. I was so angry. How dare she say that in front of Ken? How dare she get angry with me? I was just trying to look out for her, but no, she couldn't accept that I had changed and grown. I reached up and grabbed her obnoxious finger and twisted it away. "Can't handle the new Koi, huh?"

Shit. When did I switch back to English?

Ken cleared his throat. "Koi might be experiencing a bit of dream eating blowback from Elise. It makes her cranky."

At the sound of Elise's name, Pete's eyes widened. He propelled himself off the couch, reaching for Marlin's long ponytail. He yanked her back against his chest and gripped her around the throat.

"What the hell—" The rest of Marlin's words were cut off by Pete's hand, along with her air.

Ken stood up, both hands raised in the air. "You don't want to harm her." His face morphed slightly into the genial salesman features he used to manipulate people.

I was not feeling reasonable. Whether it was dream-eating crankiness or just that I'd had enough of people hurting Marlin, it didn't matter. Pete no longer deserved the chance to explain. He was hurting my sister.

Not this time, cracker. I threw myself forward on a wave of red-hazed anger and lunged for Pete's skinny white ankle above his tube socks. As soon as my fingers brushed bare skin, I held on with all my might, stretched out on Marlin's super-soft carpet. "Let her go," I said to his stinky foot.

"You're fucking crazy," Pete said, and kicked at my face. I narrowly missed a broken nose by rolling out of the way, losing my grip. But the other hand still touched bare skin.

Burn, little flame, burn.

For the first time in my life I deliberately let loose the Baku hunger that was at my core on a human. It burned hot and bright and hungry and wrenched a dream fragment from Pete. There was a confusing clamor of angry male voices and the heat of a torch in front of my face, and then his fragment was gone, burned to ashes in an instant. *More.* I tightened my grip around Pete's leg and willed the hungry flame to flare hotter.

Pete thrust Marlin away from him with a whimper, crumpling

forward at the waist to scramble frantically at my fingers. I held on, ripping another fragment from him: a flash of a beautiful blonde woman with an ugly grimace on her mouth, wooden spoon upraised to come smashing down on my obediently outstretched hand. *Mine.* That one went to the Baku flame with an aftertaste of burnt bacon and salty tears. Still I wanted more. This paltry human dreaming was nothing, I could consume it forever and still hunger. Burning, I reached for more.

But someone was squishing my cheeks in a punishing grip, and another person was tugging on my clothed arm and crying, and someone else moaned low in their throat. I blinked, the red haze lifting, twin spikes of nascent migraine piercing my temples. I was still stretched out on my belly, but now Pete was next to me, a pale limp mannequin, the slight rise and fall of his chest the only sign he still lived.

Ken released my face as soon as he saw me blinking in confusion, but Marlin continued tugging on my arm. It was her sobs I heard. I released Pete's ankle and pushed myself up to a sitting position. The world did a wobbly dance that my stomach echoed. Marlin fell on her behind, crab walking away from me, a terrified expression on her face. "What did you do to him? What did you do?"

CHAPTER TWELVE

Ken led Marlin into the bathroom, came back out, checked Pete's pulse, and tied the unconscious man's hands together with a curtain rope in a scarily efficient manner. He looked down at me on the floor. I was still breathing heavily, eyes narrowed against the migraine blooming in my skull. "I didn't mean to, I didn't."

Ken hunkered down on his heels. "*Daijyobu*, Koi-chan. *Daijoybu*."

Okay? Oh no, it most definitely was not *daijyobu*. Marlin saw me. She saw me wrenching those fragments from Pete like the monster I was. It would never be *daijyobu* ever again.

"Pete's human," I said. "He's *human*."

"What did you expect would happen coming in here with our suspicions? He went after Marlin. What would you do differently?"

"Not kill him?"

"He's not dead," said Ken with a hint of exasperation. He stood up and went into the kitchen. I heard the freezer drawer open and shut, and then he was placing ice rolled up in a towel of blessed coolness across my forehead. "And your sister just needs a moment with the bathroom mirror to see the ugly bruise marks forming on her throat to realize why you did what you did."

I took a deep breath. "If I hadn't lunged like a rabid dog, would you have done this in a gentler way?"

Ken brushed the back of his palm on my cheek. The spot was still tender from his punishing grip—necessary to keep me from becoming a murderer. His gentle touch didn't last long enough for the danger of a fragment. He meant it as a gesture of trust. The breath I'd been holding came out of me in a whoosh. It was the fearful part of me, I knew, but in that moment I wanted to kiss him, lose myself in the reassurance of his warmth and acceptance. *Would it really be such a terrible idea?*

Pete groaned and tried to roll over and sit up at the same time.

"Stop," said Ken in English.

Pete reared back with a roar and then whipped his head forward flinging a globule of phlegmy spit on Ken's cheek. My judicious Kitsune wiped it with a sleeve. "You are human and weak," said Ken matter-of-factly. "You realize we are not."

"Fucking slant-eyed fairy bastard!"

Marlin came in from the bathroom just as Pete yelled. She wobbled herself over to the armchair where she dropped, her face pale and lips pressed tightly like she was holding back nausea. Pete didn't even glance her direction but continued ranting and cursing and insulting Ken and I every which way imaginable.

I looked away, cheeks hot. "Make him stop, please."

Ken again got up, went back to the kitchen, and returned with Marlin's Cutco boning knife. She was serious about cooking and kept it sharp as a razor. Ken flashed it under Pete's nose. "Shut up."

Pete was so startled he broke off mid-curse. He licked his lips, eyes trolling the room wildly, chest heaving. "I'm not afraid of that."

Ken sighed and put the knife down on the floor just out of Pete's reach. He looked from the knife to Pete, daring him to make a break for it. Pete settled back on the floor. "I won't tell you bastards a thing. It's us or you. Blood and soil."

Marlin gasped. She leaned forward. "That's a Nazi slogan. But...but...you are..."

Pete's mouth hardened into a grim line, upper lip curling in a sneer. "Not a mongrel coolie whore."

Marlin gasped again. She blinked away wetness shining at the corner of her eyes. "Why? How could you be with me?"

"Intel, and a little bit of fun. You liked my big, thick Aryan—"

Marlin lunged forward and slapped him full across the mouth.

Pete laughed.

At that moment, I hated him more than anything on Earth for the way Marlin cringed on her knees before him. I reached for the knife.

"Let me handle it," said Ken.

I put the knife back on the floor. "He's dirt," I said, inching closer to Marlin.

"At least I'm human dirt," said Pete. "And your sister loved my dirty cock."

Marlin stopped me with an open palm. "Get back. I'm not ready to be civil with you yet."

"Language," said Ken to Pete. "I'm going to ask you some questions now and you are going to answer them without upsetting Marlin or Koi anymore."

Pete laughed again. "I'm not afraid of you. Even fairy freaks bleed. Learned that fact at the Witch's Hut."

He locked eyes with me, his mouth widening into a grin that left the pale blue empty pools of his iris untouched and cold. "The whole world is a dream," he said in a slimy, knowing tone, "and death is the interpreter." *Oh god.* I couldn't deny that those quotes were aimed at me anymore. *He knows what I am.*

Ken turned feral. Eyes narrowed into slits of hard obsidian, cheekbones sharp enough to draw blood and hands curved into claws. Quarter inch long thick nails the color of old ivory extended from his fingertips. I'd only seen them once before when Mangasar Hayk the psycho murdering PCC professor threatened my life. I wasn't sure if they were real or part of the Kitsune illusion but those claws jolted me. It was like Wolverine was in my sister's living room, only disturbingly sexier because it was real. When he went feral, all my hoarded hurts, the betrayal and anger I felt in Japan fell away, torn to shreds by the undeniably fierce presence of Fujiwara Kennosuke, Kitsune, Bringer for the Council. On *my* side.

Focus on the maniac on the floor, Survivalist Koi snapped, fighting the tide of hangry irritation the Baku inside me got from being offered the paltry, stale dreams of human scum when I'd feasted so recently on the luscious power of Yukiko-sama, the snow woman, and the ancient anguish of the Black Pearl.

While I was having a mental moment, Ken uncoiled his long limbs and spread palms across Pete's chest. The asshole's nostrils flared wide.

"What do you want with a Baku?" Ken asked.

"Baku?" Pete squeaked. He was hyperventilating.

Ken lifted his index finger like playing a piano and stabbed into Pete's flesh through the gray Henley. Pete grunted. Immediately the cotton darkened with seeping blood. *Real claws. Not illusion, real.*

"What do you want with a dream eater?"

"What are you planning to do?" my sister said. "You can't...don't..."

Ken lifted his middle finger. "This is just a flesh wound. He killed Dzunukwa and left her displayed for their grotesque amusement. He deserves far worse."

"Faggot fairy can't kill me even if you wanted to. I know your weakness," said Pete.

"Ah," said Ken, he stabbed his middle finger into Pete's chest. Another dark circle appeared. Pete screeched, turned an alarming shade of white, his eyes rolling up for a moment. Ken slapped him, and his eyes refocused. "That's where your informant let you down. Didn't they explain about me?" Ken leaned down so his face was a bare centimeter from Pete's. He smiled, revealing long, sharp canines worthy of a vampire. "I'm special. I'm the Bringer of Death."

Was the Bringer of Death. Ken didn't mention he'd quit the Council not two days before.

Marlin whimpered. "Please, I can't stand this. I cared for him."

Pete laughed, a high hyena sound.

In Dad's Northern Aomori dialect I addressed her. "Ken won't really kill him. This is our best chance to get some answers."

"Lying faggot. Suck my dick."

Ken growled and raised his entire right hand, stabbing all five fingers at once into Pete's chest. The ragged man howled, his body tensing like a bow and arching off the ground. He sobbed, gasping.

"Ah, Ken?" I wasn't so sure now that what I'd told Marlin was true. Ken was really *angry.*

"Who told you about the dream eater?" Ken's voice was growly in a way that made hairs stand up on the back of my neck.

Pete shook his head. The front of his Henley was soaked in blood. He wasn't going to talk. And I was afraid of how far Ken would go in order to break him.

"Don't," I said. "Please."

Marlin jumped in. "Can't we just take him to the police, like we did with Professor Hayk?"

Ken scoffed. "The police will do nothing. Dzunukwa does not officially exist and Elise won't report her attack. We will take him to the bonfire." He pulled back and shook himself like a dog emerging from the Columbia River. Pete's Henley was suddenly pristine gray, soaked only at the armpits with nervous sweat.

"What the?" Pete's eyes widened even further. Ken cracked his knuckles, devoid of any sign of wicked claws.

Illusion after all. Damn good one.

Since when was Ken that strong? My Kitsune plopped down on Marlin's sofa. Red spots appeared high on his cheeks. Okay, so maybe he wasn't that strong. He looked exhausted.

Marlin glanced between the two men, the desire to go to Pete's side blatant in the way she bit her quivering lower lip. Even a Nazi asshole couldn't rip the caretaker out of my sister's heart.

"Come on Maru-chan," I said to my sister, tugging on her elbow. "Let Ken take care of this mess. Let's go pack an overnight bag. You're going to come stay with us until Kwaskwi can take care of Pete's friends."

"I don't like the way you say take care of."

"He's Nordvast Uffheim. The FBI has them on their violent offender watch list."

I herded Marlin into her bedroom, throwing a stern glance over my shoulder that I hoped Ken interpreted correctly as an order to get Pete all sorted before my sister had a complete breakdown. The last time that happened she'd called the police. That hadn't ended well at all.

"I'm such a fool," said Marlin, sitting on the edge of her perfectly made bed. I sat down next to her and put an arm around her shoulders. She startled. "Who are you and what have you done with my sister?"

I fake laughed. "Yeah, all this Kind stuff is pretty freaky, but it's sort of…good for me, you know? I'm not so afraid of what I am."

"I'm afraid of what you are."

I dropped my arm. "I'm still Koi."

"I know. *Bakayarou.*" It was the Japanese equivalent of *stupid head*; a name Dad had called us in fond exasperation. "What did you do to Pete back there?"

I inventoried her expression, trying to see if she really truly wanted answers or for me to come up with some plausible explanation she could believe instead. But this wasn't the direction I wanted to go anymore with Marlin. No more Queen of Denial for me. "I forced a dream fragment from him and then I ate it."

Marlin gripped the bedspread in both hands, upsetting the perfectly symmetrical pile of satin pillows at the head. In a shaky voice she whispered, "I can't believe you answered me."

"You're overbearing and bossy," I said. I cocked my head. "And your taste in television and boyfriends suck. I mean, come on, Leverage? Just, you know, in the interest of being completely open and honest."

The corner of Marlin's mouth quirked up. Her obsession with becoming an extra for any show filmed in Portland was my favorite topic to tease her about. "Yeah, well, I've been watching a lot more Grimm these days."

"You have always been my bedrock. In the middle of all that Kind stuff, the dreams and the illusions and the dragons like Ullikemi, it's you and Dad that I kept coming back to."

Marlin breathed in slowly, shock denying her words. Me, the Queen of Denial, avoided saying stuff like this like the plague. She was my anchor, and I would do anything to protect her. To protect Dad. Even force fragments from Nazi bastards. Morbanoid Koi piped up. *And what if Kwaskwi asks me to force a fragment from an innocent human like Brian to protect Marlin? What about morals then?*

I shivered. So far I hadn't had to make that choice.

"You are my sister," said Marlin, in a way that meant we would work out the Pete torture thing somehow. She gave a sad smile. "I just wish," she swallowed something stuck in her throat, "that Mom was here."

"Yeah," I said, flashing back to that day in the hospital near the end when Mom talked about why she named me Koi—because to her carp were strong, long-lived survivors. "I think she kind of knew."

"Probably," said Marlin. "She was the one who married Dad in the first place." She got up and went to her closet, snagged a floral overnight bag from the top shelf and began opening drawers. I shook my head. Even her underwear was neatly folded. And arranged by color. A few minutes later her overnight bag was ready.

Her chest rose with a fortifying breath. "Okay," said the

overbearing, bossy, obsessive-compulsive center of my heart. "Time to face the music."

"Anyone would have fallen for Pete's seduction," I said softly. "Thus, the term 'seduction'."

"You wouldn't have," she said sharply. "Ken is the first guy I've seen you let past your defenses since high school hormones. I always pitied that. How you were alone. But now I see how tempting it would be to put the same kind of defenses around my heart."

"It's going to be okay," I said.

"It's going to get worse, first, though."

CHAPTER THIRTEEN

Ken contacted Kwaskwi about Pete. There was a curt conversation where Kwaskwi shouted through the phone and Ken maintained a tightly reined-in composure. Marlin fiddled with making latte in her fusty stove-top Bialetti Moka just so her hands were occupied, her face growing as colorless as the skim milk.

George and Henry showed up in the Subaru and bundled a protesting Pete into their car with a bag over his head mafia-style while Ken walked alongside providing an illusion of mist so none of Marlin's neighbors would freak out.

Henry tried to convince Ken we should skip going back to the hotel. "Kwaskwi already knows you're at the—"

George elbowed his brother sharply in the ribs and jerked his chin towards the car where Pete lay in the backseat.

I slapped my forehead with a palm. "The jays," I said. "Duh. He probably has one watching Dad, too."

"We will show up tonight on time. I have given my word to Kwaskwi," said Ken, directing his comments to George. That must have satisfied both Bear Brothers because they took off with their still-protesting charge quickly after that. I was *pretty* sure Kwaskwi wouldn't do anything too terrible to Pete but the horrified Survivalist in me that had tasted oily, bitter *wrongness* at the memory of Dzunukwa splayed in grotesque, wasted death didn't seem to care what Kwaskwi did with Pete. As long as he didn't harm anyone else.

My morals hung by an unraveling thread. I was closer than ever to becoming the monster I feared. Pete was *human*. Like Brian. But unlike Brian, he'd been a part of taking a life. Not that Dzunukwa was entirely innocent. But she was no threat to Pete, the Nordvast Uffheim or any other humans living in Portland.

"Time to go," said Ken, a warm hand landing on the middle of my lower back, urging me towards our favorite taxi that had just pulled up, right on time. Marlin came down the stairs with her overnight bag. We slid into the back seat.

"I always wanted to stay at the Heathman," she said. "Do you think the doorman would let me wear his hat?"

I closed my eyes and shook my head in mock disapproval. Was I the only person here not obsessed with Beefeaters? "You're going to have to be careful for a few days," I said.

"No social media, no telling anyone where you are," said Ken from the front seat. "No driving your own car."

"I've got appointments with clients tomorrow and Tuesday," said Marlin.

Ken twisted around. "Did Pete have access to your calendar? Does he know your clients?"

"Yeah, he did."

"Reschedule."

"I guess I could do that."

I squeezed Marlin's knee. "This stuff kind of sucks. But it's necessary."

"What about Dad?"

I heaved a sigh. "As long as you didn't mention in front of Pete where he is staying, he's probably okay for a while with Nurse Jenny."

"That's not what I'm asking about."

I dug my thumbs into my temples. Creeping, feathery fingers of pain were brushing over my skull. "The medic in Japan said he may never wake up."

"Goddammit Koi."

"I'm sorry. I just wanted you to be prepared for the worst."

"How am I supposed to be prepared for never being able to talk to him again? For losing another parent?"

"He's lived a long life," I said, weighing how much of what I'd learned about Dad to explain. His service in Japan's army occupying Manchuria during World War II, his sister, and the possibility he'd been alive since the Edo Shogunate. "He survived World War II and immigrating to the United States. He's a tough old coot." *And unimaginably powerful Baku.*

"Let's go right now. I need to see him, Koi."

I understood how she felt. Something in me believed if both his daughters went to him together, he would awaken out of that coma. *Silly, foolish belief.*

Ken bowed his head and shook it. "It might not be a good idea to draw attention to him."

"Pete's far away. I want to see Dad, too." I said. Marlin's eyes lit up. "There's a chance," my breath caught, "I haven't tried to enter his dreaming. Maybe…maybe I could contact him somehow. Ask him about all this Nordvast Uffheim stuff."

"Koi," said Ken, imbuing my name with pity-laced anxiety.

I'm running to Daddy. I guess maybe it's not such a hot idea right this minute. "Okay, I can wait."

Marlin scoffed. "So, I'm supposed to just sit in a hotel room while you two go out, and what, round up Neo-Nazis?"

"You probably should power off your phone now, too," said Ken.

Marlin pierced Ken with her fiercest glare. "You have got to be kidding."

"We can't be sure what kind of technology they have."

Marlin pulled out her phone and did as Ken asked. "I'm going to get a temporary phone," she said. Her voice dripped with sarcasm. "If that's okay with you, Ken." She was an emotional Yo-Yo. I guess even highly organized planners didn't know how to deal with finding out their boyfriend was Nazi scum.

Marlin turned away, staring out the window. She said nothing until the taxi pulled up in front of the Heathman, and then her whole attitude changed. She burst out of the taxi, stealing my phone to snap her selfies with the doorman—a different, younger and way more muscled one than had posed with Ken. Ken paid the taxi driver and arranged for him to pick us up again in an hour.

"Why use a taxi?" I said to Ken after it pulled away. "Kwaskwi knows where we are. Why not just let George and Henry pick us up?"

"Instinct," he said. "It feels safer this way."

Marlin oohed and awed over the opulent lobby, the dark wood paneling, and the carpet color in the hallway. She entered the Warhol suite and stopped dead in her tracks. "Damn, girl. This is hella swank." She beelined for the bathroom and shut the door with a loud click. After a moment I heard the gurgling flow of the shower turning on.

"Well that went well," I said, slumping into a chair. I hugged the chair cushion over my belly. "I particularly enjoyed *slant-eyed fairy bastard*."

"I've never been called that before," said Ken, utterly serious.

"What next?"

"This bonfire will be the first time the Portland community will see you. It's important to make a good impression. A strong impression."

"Why does it matter?"

Ken came and sat on the sofa's edge. "Kwaskwi put himself in a difficult position. His first attempt to acquire your father ended with him almost losing Thunderbird to you and Ullikemi. Leaving

Portland to follow you to Japan made it clear he was throwing the weight of his power and that of the Portland Kind behind you."

"I thought he came to Japan to treat with the Council."

Ken scoffed. "He helped us in Aomori against the Council's objectives. It's clear that he's willing to risk the Council's anger because you and your father are more important."

"Right."

Ken knelt next to the ottoman. His turned-up face was devoid of any levity. This was deadly serious territory. "Kwaskwi's motives lie in something deeper than just getting your help with these attacks, Koi." He glanced down at my hands, twisted on top of the pillow. "May I?" he reached for my right hand.

I nodded. His strong, slender fingers were cool on my worried, heated flesh. He cupped my hand in both of his and bent to brush his lips across the back of my knuckles. It was old-fashioned and strangely powerful, stoking up a banked heat deep in my middle. A flash of the fragment I always got from Ken—running in a cool, moonlit primal forest of ferns with *hinoki* cypress towering overhead —washed over me in a delicious shiver. I welcomed the fragment as an old friend, allowing a tiny flare of my Baku flame to burn through it. Tingles spread from my belly down my arms and legs. The nascent migraine flitted away.

Ken had gone feral Kitsune again when he lifted his head from my hand. His Japanese was formal and nuanced with old-fashioned honorifics. "The Council lost Yukiko-sama and the Black Pearl's ambient magic. Tojo is a raging bull. That leaves only Kawano-sama to retain control of the entire Pacific Basin region. With Thunderbird and you on his side, Kwaskwi is more powerful."

The words broke the pleasant interlude of Ken's fragment buzz. A hot rush of fear flushed down my back. "Me?" I squeaked.

"You," said Ken. He kissed my knuckles again while I sat, frozen in shock, thinking about the implications of Kwaskwi as leader of the Pacific Basin Kind. Of power shifting from Tokyo to Portland. Ken pulled out a pen knife. He flicked it open and sliced a small opening in his palm. Blood welled, sluggish and red. "I pledge myself, Fujiwara Kennosuke, to you. To the Baku Pierce Herai Koi AweoAweo." He pressed his bleeding palm flush with mine.

Something slid into place inside my ribcage, lodging there like a grappling hook as the hotel room spun 360 degrees. And I was in Ken's forest again. Cypress needles rustled under my feet, releasing their biting scent into the air. Cool ferns brushed my back as I ran, elated, excited. I came to a full stop at the edge of a clearing. There, under a far tree stood a woman. She had long, dark brown hair with copper highlights that glinted under the moon like she was bathed in warm sunlight instead, a stance that spoke of strength, a jaw that spoke of determination, and my heart was so full of her that it nearly burst from my chest. Every cell in my body yearned towards her, like she was a lodestone and I a lost wanderer.

What did you do, Ken?

This was his old, familiar fragment, but with the addition of me. Or at least a version of Koi he must have dreamed many times for her to appear so vibrantly alive. My Baku flame flared to life before I could react, hungry, *wanting*. Ken was Kind and this dream seductively powerful.

I ate the dream, the flame burning through the cypress, the vision of me, and even the silken moonlight in the space of a breath. Power thrilled through my veins, buzzing and fizzing, and the desire to keep going, to burn and burn and burn until all of Ken's life energy flowed through my body was a fierce, aching joy.

It was the blood. Adding blood power to his pledge and then offering himself to the ravenous Baku. *As a sacrifice? No.* We'd played this game before and he lost. I would not be his vehicle for self-destruction. Someone, somewhere cried out in pain.

I grit my mental teeth and willed my flame to dim. Slowly, slowly the greens and shadowed blues of the forest faded into the air, leaving behind a grey wall of static.

The static swirled as if caught in a hurricane funnel and then spun out in all directions, revealing the fuchsia drapes and rainbow Marilyn Monroe paintings of the Warhol suite. Ken knelt still on the floor beside me, dripping with sweat and heaving great gasps of air.

I wrenched my hand away. "What are you trying to prove?"

"You haven't trusted me since Tokyo," said Ken in a breathy rasp. "Now you can have no doubt."

"It's not just you I don't trust. *Bakayaroo.*"

Ken's furrowed brow and tight jaw did not loosen.

"What if I hurt you?" I asked so softly I wasn't sure the words carried to Ken's ears. But he tightened his fists on his thighs. I'd disconnected from his dream fragment, but that odd sense of something inside my ribcage remained. It was the feeling of Ken, the heaviness of his presence connected to me by his pledge and his blood. And *oh god*, now that it was there, I never wanted to be without it again.

I turned away, unwilling for him to read anything in my eyes. "I didn't ask for this."

"No matter. I am bound to serve and protect you now," said Ken. "The Council, Kwaskwi, no one can interfere with the pledge. You are my mission now. You and your father. I will accept whatever role you choose for me." He glanced up at me from underneath those long, thick lashes and arched an eyebrow. "Of course," he added in English, "I would prefer an intimate one."

That damn eyebrow. It melted me into mush. A smile threatened to lift the corners of my severe frown. Before I could come up with a retort or even begin to decide what I felt about him tricking this on me, Marlin half opened the bathroom door. "Safe to come out? Everyone decent?"

I cleared my throat. Ken rose in one, long, liquid movement from his knees and arranged his long limbs in a casual sprawl on the sofa just as Marlin, wrapped in towels, emerged from the bathroom. "Your turn," she said, and headed for the bedroom.

I didn't dare look at Ken as I fled to the bathroom. It was steamy and warm from Marlin's shower. I wiped a clear spot in the vanity mirror and leaned over the sink, considering my own face. The face of someone who inspired magical beings to slice themselves up and pledge their lives should be more regal. Less pudgy about the cheeks. And definitely should not be stuck in an expression of annoyed puzzlement.

I held a ridiculously luxurious monogrammed washcloth under the cold water faucet and pressed it to my forehead. The sensation rooted me in a stronger sense of my body's physicality. I wiped away the fog of confusion resulting from eating Ken's dream. If I was brutally honest with myself, the tender parts of my heart, still a bit raw from the way Ken withdrew into his Council Bringer role in Japan, ached less. He wanted me. He trusted me. So much that he bound himself to me in a formal Kind way I probably didn't fully appreciate. I cupped my hands underneath the flow and messily gulped cold, copper-scented water, seized with a fierce thirst.

I wanted Ken. I could forgive him and try again. The odd heaviness in my ribcage settled into a comfortable, pleasant feeling of warmth.

"Koi!" Ken's voice held a note of urgency.

I turned off the faucet and went back out into the sitting room part of the suite. Ken held his cell phone at eye level. It was a pic sent by text from Kwaskwi's phone. In it, George or Henry's large, hairy hand, streaked with dark crimson, dangled from the smashed window of the Subaru. The front of the car was crumpled against a black minivan.

"There's been another attack."

CHAPTER FOURTEEN

"Give me leave to go," said Ken urgently.

"What?"

Ken growled in frustration. "This just happened. They might still be near the scene of the crime. I shouldn't interfere with Portland Kind business unless I do it in your name. *Give me leave to go.*"

"Yes, sure, ah…go."

Ken went feral. Behind me Marlin gave a startled shriek. I stumbled back a few steps. Ken had gone full-blown Kitsune before, but this was different. His eyes rolled up into his head. After a couple rapid blinks, there was no trace of white at all. His cheekbones could have cut glass and when he shook himself all over like a dog, his hair appeared shaggier and his canines more pronounced. He spun and was through the door before the dropped phone reached the plush carpet.

"What the hell was that? Is he a werewolf?"

"Kitsune," I said, bending over to retrieve the phone. There was another pic. It showed Henry lying on his back a few feet from the car. It was George's hand dangling from the window, but there was no sign at all of Pete in the back seat. *Thrown from the car and dead?*

"Pete might have escaped."

Marlin slid to the floor and put her head between her knees, hyperventilating. I knelt beside her and smoothed the hair behind her ear, letting my hand rest in the middle of her back. "I have to go, too," I said.

"No!" Her eyes widened in the middle of a blotchy face. "Stay here with me!"

"I can't."

"Why you?"

Because I owe Kwaskwi. Because Ken is putting himself in danger. Because this threatens Dad and you. None of the reasons felt exactly like the truth. Dzunukwa was a fearful creature. Her death was startling and scary, but it didn't touch my inner heart. Elise was a bitch, but she didn't deserve to be targeted by whacko Nazi-wannabes. George and Henry were altogether different. I'd ridden in their Subaru. I'd seen how George looked after his brother and the eager puppy way Henry tried to talk to everyone. Despite being at odds with them the first time we met, they'd become friends. And someone hurt them.

Like a squiggly Venn diagram, I drew a line around the increasing number of people in the world important to me. Somewhere within that group was an even smaller circle, the nucleus of my family cell: Dad, Marlin, Kwaskwi, and Ken.

Dad. All alone. If the Nordvast Uffheim had identified and risked messing with the Bear Brothers, then he might be in more danger than I thought.

Crazy Nazis would not hurt anyone else in my circle.

"Marlin," I said. "I changed my mind. Let's go see Dad, but I need your help first."

Marlin gave a sobbing laugh. "What can I do?"

This bonfire will be the first time the Portland community will see you. It's important to make a good impression. A strong impression.

Kwaskwi put all his eggs in the Baku basket. A pang shot through me. When he'd asked for my help before, with Brian, I'd refused. Would Elise and the Bear Brothers have been attacked if I bent my scruples a little? Would I have seen Pete in Brian's dreams?

"I need you to make me over. Give me that professional mask you put on for trade shows."

Marlin stared at me with her tongue pressed into one cheek like Mom when she was analyzing research data. "For this bonfire thing? Why?"

"Kwaskwi won't sit idly by while humans pick off his people one by one. He's gearing up for something big at this bonfire, I just know it. I may be the best chance we have to stop a human Kind war."

CHAPTER FIFTEEN

After a three-minute shower, Marlin wound my hair in a towel and sat me down on an easy chair. She plucked and brushed and shaped and contoured. I'd never had so much product on my face before— and this was all from Marlin's travel kit.

There was no call from Kwaskwi or Ken no matter how many times I checked my phone. Texts went unanswered except for a terse *busy* from Ken. I even called Pon-suma, but unsurprisingly he wasn't answering, either.

"Bend over so I can blow dry your hair," Marlin commanded. I bent over while Marlin scrunched mousse into my hair. When I was finally allowed right side up, I felt a little light-headed from heat and fumes and blood rushing to my head.

"Okay, go look in the mirror," said Marlin after a few strategic shots of hairspray. "I'll try to whip up something for you to wear."

I went into the bathroom swiping my phone for the millionth time. At last! A text from Pon-suma came in Japanese.

Pete escaped. We lost attackers. George and Henry critical. Bonfire still on. Ken says come by taxi and don't do anything stupid.

He will meet you at the gate.

Got it. I'm coming. You okay?

Ok.

I glanced at the mirror, relieved, and did a double take. The same old brown eyes with the slight epicanthic fold stared back, but somehow Marlin had drawn wings with eyeliner and curled my lashes so that they looked huge. Shaded variations of grey eye shadow accentuated what I'd inherited from Japanese DNA and made my eyelids look as big as Mom's Caucasian ones. She'd outlined my lips in a darker plum liner I'd never have the courage to try on my own. I'd pictured my hair in a professional chignon or French braid, but Marlin's decision to let it float around my head in long waves contrasted with the sleek makeup, conveying both competence and guilelessness.

Neither of those adjectives really were the truth. *Ha. Try bewildered and freakish.*

I went back out to the sitting room to tell Marlin the news. After a moment I realized she was carefully applying the same wings and lip liner she'd used on me to her own face. "Dad won't care if you have lipstick on."

She swiveled in the chair and fixed me with her patented 200-megawatt death glare. I blinked, stifling the urge to rub my eyes and mess up all her hard work. "I'm going with you to the bonfire, too."

"No way!"

"I can't just sit here alone in this hotel."

"This is dangerous."

"You're going," she said through gritted teeth.

"I'm Baku."

"My father and sister are Baku! All of this terrifies me, Koi. But Pete hurt me. He made me feel like a fool just to get at you. I need to be a part of this. You can't keep shoving me away from the most important parts of your life!"

I sighed, chains of worry tightening around my ribcage. Marlin was as stubborn as a pit-bull with a chew toy. The bonfire was the one place, though, where there would be other people who would care enough to keep her safe. Ken, Pon-suma, and even Kwaskwi would be around. Plus, the idea of having Marlin with me at a social function where I had to meet a crap ton of strangers and convince them that it wasn't a good idea to hunt down and kill racist humans did have some appeal.

At least Marlin would remember everyone's name.

"Okay."

"Really?"

"You can come, but you have to stick close to Ken or Pon-suma."

Marlin scrunched up her nose. "I don't know Pon-suma that well. I'm sure he's nice, but why can't I stick with you?"

"Dire things keep happening to me these days."

"I'll risk it," said Marlin, slinging an arm across my shoulders in a sideways squeeze. We exchanged startled, matching wing-eye glances and then broke apart.

A hug was a simple thing. People hugged every day without much thought. Even so, Marlin would not have attempted a hug on me even three weeks ago, considering the touch aversion I had before I learned to control dream fragments.

My sister had ransacked the lobby gift shop while I showered and used her magical powers to produce an outfit to go with the hair and makeup. She lent me a pair of her black leggings and knee-high black leather boots with just-manageable two-inch heels. A sleeveless, wine colored velvet shift dress with a way plungy neckline went on top.

"Let me put this velvet choker on you," she said.

"That might be where I draw the line. I'm not going for sexy dream eater. I'm going for take me seriously bad-ass Baku. Also, this is a bonfire. Outside. I can't wear my hoodie with this."

She smiled wide, striding over to her overnight bag. "I have just the thing." She pulled out a black leather jacket with wide lapels. It balanced out the feminine dress perfectly. I still felt like an extra in a

Katy Perry video, but this version of me would definitely make a strong impression.

"Okay." I heaved a sigh. "Let's go see Dad."

We left the hotel room together, Marlin closing the door with a wistful expression. On South Broadway in front of the Heathman, people streamed towards the brick haven of Pioneer Square dressed either in tourist casual or plaid hipster. Across the street, women in cocktail dresses and men in short-sleeved shirts rolled up to reveal muscles and tattoos lingered around the Artbar bistro tables. It was a normal night, and these were normal people. But my eyes lingered on all the blonde men's tattoos, scanning for arrow crosses or the number 14.

Marlin stepped in front of me. "What are you doing?"

"Being morbanoid."

"Stop staring at the guests. You're making Keith uncomfortable."

"Keith?"

"Him," she said, pointing at the Beefeater who was opening a taxi door for a thin man in a white Arab long thobe tunic. Keith winked at Marlin. He gave me a curious look.

Ah. Keith probably didn't get good tips if a psycho woman was standing outside the hotel leering at men's forearms. Luckily, a more familiar taxi soon pulled up to the curb. My favorite Sikh driver rolled the window down and exchanged a few words with Keith. This resulted in Marlin and I jumping the taxi line, to the disapproving stares of a few elderly women sporting Coach purses and multiple diamond rings.

Marlin somehow did that smooth thing where she gave Keith folded up bills as he handed her into the backseat of the taxi. Keith kept a level smile as I slid in next to her, but thankfully didn't try to help in any other way than closing the taxi door.

"Where to?" said the driver. It struck me that I'd spent more time in his taxi than in my own apartment since returning to the States. The worn black vinyl seemed plain after the white doily covered taxis

I just experienced in Tokyo, but it was comforting and familiar. I ran my hand over the pebbled surface of the seat. "Cedar Sinai Park Adult Center."

Marlin told the driver the address. We passed the short trip in silence. My stomach gurgled with what felt like car-sickness, but was probably more like *what if Dad never woke up* and *what if Pete knew he was a Baku* sickness. Marlin led the way through Cedar Sinai's side door to the private room areas. Nurse Jenny had gone home for the day, but at the nurse's desk a young, blond-haired nurse seemed to recognize Marlin. She took us straight away to Dad's room. *If I'd showed up in hoodie and messy ponytail would the nurse have been as trusting?*

I half expected clicking and beeping machines and the swoosh of a breathing apparatus like in all the TV shows and movies. But the only signs Dad wasn't just asleep were an IV and a saline bag hanging above the bed. Marlin went to the bedside chair and took Dad's hand with a gesture that cut me to the quick with its casual confidence. She'd never been able to take my hand like that. Dad had control over his dream eating. He could have spent the last decade teaching instead of keeping me ignorant about my nature. *Ah well, if I'm the Queen of Denial, he's the Emperor.*

Blondie Nurse took his pulse and felt his forehead, making a note on a chart hanging at the foot of the bed. She closed the drapes on the double windows. "There's been no change since he arrived. He hasn't regained consciousness, but his vital signs are steady and strong. I'll leave you for a short visit, then. Just stop by the desk to check out when you go," she said. Marlin and I nodded.

"Now what?"

I went to the other side of the bed. In sleep, Dad's face relaxed into a smooth mask, making him appear younger and innocent. "Now I see if he'll let me into his dreams."

Marlin settled into the chair. "Do I need to do anything? Like pull your hand off him if you aren't back in a few minutes? Keep an eye on his heartbeat?"

I shrugged. "I wish I knew more about this, but I don't. I can tell you that in Japan, I gained a bit more control over experiencing other's dreams. But Dad...he's been Baku far longer than me. He could block me out if he wanted."

"Okay then."

"Here goes nothing." I put my palm to Dad's cheek.

The world spun and when it righted itself, the white walls shimmered and darkened into a blank room. Seamless grey walls merged into a cold concrete floor.

What are you doing here?

I turned and there was Dad, crouching in his blue Japanese Manchukuo army uniform, heavy brows drawn together in anger.

CHAPTER SIXTEEN

Dad. Are you okay?

He shook his head, springing to his feet with arms outstretched. He grabbed both sides of my army uniform collar and twisted, choking off air. *I'm wearing a uniform too?*

I will not. I will not. I will not, he repeated, each time giving me a little shake.

Dad!

He blinked, his hands falling away as the room turned into the sushi counter at Marinopolis. The army uniform bleached into a white chef's jacket and the Marinopolis tuna mascot on a bandana wound around his head *hachimaki* style.

Koi-chan?

Every detail of Dad's restaurant sans customers was in bright, vivid color. Each slat on the bamboo mat, each tassel on the silly lanterns that were actually Chinese looked exactly as I remembered. Dad expertly controlled the dreaming in a way I'd never fully appreciated. A warm feeling tickled my stomach. Marinopolis Dad was the Dad of my childhood.

You know where you are?

In Portland. Yes?

Cedar Sinai.

That's probably for the best. He perched on a tall stool.

You aren't waking up soon, are you?

I am damaged, Koi.

I swallowed a hysterical wave of protests. *There is a group of white supremacists in Portland who discovered the Kind. They've somehow latched on to Baku as public enemy number one.*

They are the ones who murdered Dzunukwa.

Yes. And attacked Elise. Wait. How did you know about Dzunukwa?

The dreaming is permeable. I occasionally hear outside conversations.

But you can't wake up?

No.

The white supremacists left really creepy death and dreaming graffiti. They called out Baku in particular. Dad didn't need to know what Pete did to Marlin.

Ah, so. Dad folded his hands and piled them on one knee. *This is what I tried to protect you from, although I did not foresee the threat coming from humans so quickly. But then, I did not foresee Mangasar Hayk or Ullikemi either.*

You knew about the white supremacists?

No. But they aren't the first human group that discovered the Kind and attempted to either destroy or use us.

Kwaskwi wanted me to force dreams from a human who saw Dzunukwa's murder for information. I couldn't.

We can guide dreams. Dad gestured at the sushi restaurant. *This is a dream I come back to often.*

I've always called them kernel dreams. The dreams someone has over and over again. The fundamental focus of their life.

Dad nodded gravely.

The sushi restaurant's walls rippled, like a stone dropped in the water of a pond. When the waves settled, we were in Marlin's apartment, and Dad was sitting on the couch. I looked around. The details here were a bit fuzzier.

How do you do that?

With practice, it becomes easier. But the first time I tried, I needed life energy. Just a cut, a small welling of blood. His lips twisted into a rueful frown. *As you eat a dream, call on your own kernel. That's the best way to start.*

I closed my eyes. Calling up my Baku-self flame. It burned steadily like a candle within me since this all started back in Ankeny Square with Ullikemi. I let it consume a little bit of Marlin's apartment. The walls rippled again. Dad let out a forceful exhale. Marlin's kernel was a high school football game. Ken's was running as a fox in a primeval forest. What I had never admitted to myself was that my kernel was the hospital where Mom died in her bed, organs consumed by mutant-tumor cells.

Marlin's trendy olive-toned walls bleached into the unforgiving white of OHSU. A wooden visitor's chair replaced the sofa under Dad, and between us, a hospital bed formed with a hazy outline of an emaciated woman.

A sharp spike of pain pierced my chest. I wasn't ready for Dad to see Mom like this. When she was near the end and he left. Abandoned our family. Just before I abandoned her as well, lest I brush bare skin and accidentally experience a death fragment—the last dream of her mortal soul as she slipped into the final dark sleep.

That's enough.

Dad's chest rose and fell in rapid breaths. Tension wrinkles lined his mouth. I released my grip on the dream and the walls went back to the grey seamless room I thought of as Dad's *neutral.*

I'm sorry.

His mouth pressed into a bloodless line. *That is not what I hoped for you.*

I shrugged. *Once I have my kernel dream, what do I do next? How do I make a person replay a memory in a dream?*

You have to have some sense of what the memory was. Details of who was there or where it was. And be careful. Memory fragments are rarely untouched by the dreamer's desires and fears.

That makes sense.

I am tired, Koi.

Dad, mom never hated you.

But he wasn't going to let me take the conversation in this direction. *It's time for you to go. Be careful. Take care of Marlin.* He turned to face a gray wall. Slowly, a spot of light blossomed, an opening to a rural landscape with a traditional thatched-roof Japanese style house.

Goodbye, Otoo-san, I said, giving him the formal *father* in Japanese I rarely did in real life.

He nodded and stepped into the light.

The gray room cracked, shattered into a million small pieces. Tossed in an unseen wind, they spun round and round, settling into a haphazard mosaic. The pieces began melting at the edges, and where they swirled together they formed a new pattern.

Marlin's face, silently crying over the body of my unconscious father in the cold reality of now.

CHAPTER SEVENTEEN

At the nurse's station Marlin confirmed no one had made inquiries after Dad. She got their promise to keep his presence here private. Only Nurse Jenny, Marlin, or I were listed as approved visitors. Our taxi was waiting outside the front doors when we exited Cedar Sinai. We slipped into the cab and asked him to take us to Lewis and Clark Recreation Area.

The driver nodded and slid into traffic.

"Here," said Marlin brandishing a tissue and an eyeliner pencil, "let me fix your face."

I told Marlin that Dad was okay, and that he'd told me a little about how to control dreams. I explained that he'd been damaged when we released the Black Pearl. This entailed more explanations about the Council in Japan and their imprisonment of an ancient dragon in Aomori since World War II. She listened with pursed lips, asking questions here and there, mostly about Pon-suma and the rebel group made up of Hafu Kind called the Eight Span Mirror. Ken's stepmother Midori, wife of the main Eight Span Mirror dude, was a normal-seeming medic who basically took care of Dad the entire time. Wheels churned in Marlin's brain.

"She was Hafu Kitsune like Ken? But she couldn't do all those crazy illusions?"

"Yeah," I said. "And she didn't shy away from confronting the Council's goons, either."

"Like me."

"Hmmm."

The pit of my stomach rebelled at the image of Marlin going up against anybody, let alone Council goons. I moved on to describing the Bear Brothers and Dzunukwa so she was solid on the Portland players as well.

"Are they Hafu?"

"Ah…I'm not sure. Elise is, though. Hafu Kobold, actually."

"What the hell is a Kobold?"

I pointed at her cell phone. "Google it." Marlin dropped down a myths and creatures research rabbit hole. She bit her lower lip, squinted at her cellphone in an adorable, near-sighted way, and left me in blessed silence for the last leg of our journey as passed the Troutdale airport and crossed over the Sandy River via the Vietnam Veterans Memorial Highway. This finger of land, caught between the spunky Sandy River on one side and the mighty Columbia on the other was verdant green in a wholesome, soul-cleansing way. I stared at the line of darkening pink cresting the tree tops, trying not to let my thoughts veer towards the disquieting reality that someone, somewhere out there, hated me for what I was by accident of birth so fiercely that they killed Dzunukwa to lure me out. How did one conceive of murderous hate? It hurt to think about, but I couldn't stop. Like worrying at a sore tooth with my tongue.

We passed a park service sign. "Pull in the entrance?" asked the driver.

"Yes, please. Can you head towards the parking lot?"

"Whatever you say, miss. Happy to oblige." He had a slight British accent that became more pronounced each time we met. For some reason that made me trust him more.

We followed a tree-lined path to a road in front of a chain-link fence. Two men stood talking next to a cute little sports car Marlin probably could identify. We pulled to a stop with a crunching spray of gravel just as I realized I still had no money.

"*Okane aru no?*" I asked Marlin.

She rolled her eyes and reached inside her blazer for her Vera Bradley lanyard. She slipped bills out of the attached id case. "Yes, I do. How did you survive in Japan without me? Seriously."

"Here's my card," said the driver. "I'm going off shift soon, but my cousin Aabi drives for Lyft."

Marlin took the card and paid while I jumped out of the car.

Ken broke away from Pon-suma and headed my way. The darkening sky painted shadows over his eyes and obscured his expression. "I've never seen you—" he closed his mouth with a click. "Your hair looks nice."

"Lame greeting, dude." He filled out his black t-shirt and blazer over tight, artfully ripped jeans pretty nicely, too. *Not telling him that.*

Ken leaned in close, nostrils flaring. "Don't punish me for withholding my real feelings. I'm trying not to push you, Koi," he said quietly, each word a flare of warmth on my cheek. "This is not the time for me to confess how much I long to stroke the soft velvet underneath that jacket. Or tell you how the beauty of your dark eyes in the moonlight makes my breath catch."

I was speechless. A little shimmery heat flushed my cheeks. My life just hadn't prepared me for smooth-tongued Japanese devils with flowery phrases.

"No, it isn't," I managed to sputter.

Ken shuffled backwards. He was clearly enjoying the effect his words had on me, but took pity and changed the subject. "You brought Marlin?"

"She insisted."

He folded his arms over his chest and sucked air through closed teeth in the same way Dad used to when I begged him for the car on Saturday nights as a teenager. "This will be overwhelming for her."

"No kidding. But she's a part of all this. Like Midori and Elise."

"Hmmm," said Ken. "Not exactly."

"Are George and Henry okay?"

"Kwaskwi took them to Providence Portland Medical Center."

"Not to Chet? Can Kind go to hospitals? Doesn't their blood show up weird on tests or something?"

Ken arched an eyebrow.

Oh, yeah. I've had blood tests my whole life. And x-rays. Stupid question.

"It seemed that Kwaskwi didn't want to involve Chet in this."

Oh ho. Point for Pon-suma.

"But they're okay?"

"Stitches and some broken bones. Apparently George has a really hard head."

"Was there…was there another quote?"

"No," said Ken. "I think this attack wasn't planned like the other ones."

Marlin came up beside me. She nodded at Ken.

"Time to go," Pon-suma called out. He'd pulled his long hair into a man bun high on the back of his head. He wore black, formal hakama trousers and a man's kimono with a crest embroidered in gold thread on the left side. I couldn't make out what it was in the dim light, but I appreciated that Pon-suma cleaned up mighty fine.

"Is this a Karmann Ghia? For real? Convertible?" Marlin said as Pon-suma held open the passenger door for her.

"1974."

"Sweet." Marlin chattered on about cars and Volkswagens while Pon-suma nodded and made his usual terse responses.

Ken and I squeezed into the back seat. "Are you ready for this? Kwaskwi is certainly going to put you on display."

"No, not really ready. But very determined."

Ken patted my knee. He reached into the side pocket of his blazer and pulled out a pair of black silk evening gloves. "You're going to have to meet quite a few Kind tonight," he said. "This is America. If it were Japan, you could get away with bowing, but here…"

My breastbone gave a twinge, as if the hook that I'd felt lodge there after Ken pledged himself to me were tugging me closer, more tightly to him.

"That is the most thoughtful thing…" I couldn't finish the thought. It was too close to confessing how desolate my life had been before Ken, before meeting the Kind. "That's very sweet." I picked up a glove, the silk was soft and cool as moonlight in my hands.

"Sweet enough for a kiss?"

"Don't push your luck." I slid my jacket off to pull on the gloves. They reached up to my elbows and fit like a second skin. *Definitely rocking the gloves in this outfit. Not freakish at all.*

Pon-suma pulled onto a path hidden behind a sharp turn in the road. We bumped over ruts and around boulders until the car's headlights illuminated a solid rock wall ahead. Broughton Bluffs. Or at least part of it. I wasn't sure if we were actually in the park anymore.

"Walk from here," said Pon-suma. He turned off the car under the dense canopy of the trees. The bluff hid the moon and instantly inky darkness swallowed us up. Pon-suma tossed Ken a flashlight, and the boys illuminated another chain-link fence. This one had large no trespassing signs and a gate locked tight with three huge padlocks.

Ken rattled the padlocks. Then, with a grin, he reached for the opposite hinge side of the gate and knocked it free with a light touch. "This way," he said, using his flashlight to usher us up a narrow, climbing footpath bound between the brooding, towering monolith of the bluff on one side and clumps of boulders studded with straggling trees on the other. My sexy boots meant keeping my gaze down or risk breaking an ankle on a root or the crumbling shale.

After ten minutes my calves burned from the climb, and I had all the regrets for the glamour shot impulse I'd had back at the hotel. I longed for my Doc Martens.

Marlin tapped me on the shoulder. "Look." She pointed to a steady red pinprick of light tucked in an overhanging rock ledge.

"Security," said Pon-suma.

"No one's getting in here without Kwaskwi knowing, one way or another." Ken picked up a rock and threw it, overhand, into the nearest tree. Immediately familiar, angry squawking broke open the quiet evening silence. Two jays rose from the tree with rapidly flapping wings and dive-bombed Ken's head. He stood firm like a statue as the jays disappeared into the darkness.

Marlin expelled a deep breath. "That was...you're saying...Kwaskwi can mind control birds?"

"Or see out of their eyes or something," I said.

Ken took the lead again. Marlin pushed my rear end up as we scrambled over a boulder. At last, the steep incline eased into a smooth, wide path under lodge pole trees. Each footstep released the sweet, sharp bite of freshly fallen pine needles.

I don't know what I was expecting, really. Hazy, cinematic images of people in medieval druid robes or torches sputtering in a magic circle while grotesque creatures out of Grimm's fairytales cavorted with tankards of ale hovered in my mind when I pictured Kwaskwi's bonfire. But I emerged from the forest onto an open plateau surrounded on three sides by the pine tops, and on a third side a sheer drop into the Sandy River back-lit by a million stars twinkling in a crushed velvet night sky. A super moon hung full and torpid, backlighting the perfect triangle of Mt. Hood. I winced at my own naiveté.

It was so much more mundane yet fantastical than my pop culture-drawn assumptions.

There was a stone altar heaped with wood and a white event tent. Two dozen or so people dressed in a range from business suits to gypsy patchwork skirts, none of whom had weird hair or claws, milled around under the fairy light lit tent, holding glass stemware filled with drinks of various colors. Another dozen lined up in front of a folding table nearby, getting nametags and handing money over to a lady dressed all in black with a white apron. At the far end of the table was a wooden T-bar stand where a giant jay perched, raking a beady eye over each guest as they passed.

Anxiety started a pot simmering in my stomach. The dress was a stupid idea. I probably looked like a child's dress up doll and the jacket sleeves pinched my upper arms. There were just so many people. All of them strangers.

"Breathe and smile," said Marlin's voice next to my ear. She cupped my elbow and moved me forward towards the table. Pon-suma and Ken bowed and said introductory things in English to the lady in black. She looked up, startled, and quickly shot a glance over Ken's shoulder, making eye contact with a burly guy standing at attention under the tent.

All of a sudden, the dull murmur of conversations all over the plateau was replaced by the rise and fall of whispers like hushed waves. All eyes fixed on our little party. Some lingered on Ken, some on Pon-suma and his man-bun, but they all eventually landed on Marlin and me.

"They're staring," I said, my voice cracking a bit high. My lips felt frozen.

"Eyes don't have the power to hurt you," said Marlin. Then she checked herself. "At least, human eyes don't. There aren't Kind with laser eyes, right?"

Something shifted in the sky, blotting out the distractingly gorgeous brilliance of the stars directly overhead. The jay on the wooden stand chattered and fluffed out its wings. Suddenly it was the only sound on the whole plateau—even the crickets shut up. In an eerie silence a band of jays descended in a swirling funnel. Moving so fast they were a blur of shiny, black feathers, one by one the jays veered off, winging over the treetops with calls that shattered the crystal silence into jagged pieces. A man was revealed as the last few tore away—Kwaskwi, of course.

Pon-suma gasped, and I choked back an exclamation, too. This was a regal Kwaskwi completely devoid of trickster bravado and the aw-shucks hayseed demeanor he usually cultivated. Or was this yet another mask? Either way, this Kwaskwi was magnificent. His hair was formed of the blackest night, cascading straight and shining down his back. Giant, silver hoops graced his ears and a diamond stud glinted from his left nostril. A pure white shirt, open to just above his navel, revealed a gleaming, well-chiseled chest above brown, skin-tight leather pants.

But it was the Eagle Feather Bonnet that took my breath away. So many feathers. I knew enough from the Cree People Googling I did the first time I met Kwaskwi that each feather represented a major deed or accomplishment. The feathers were woven together with some kind of animal sinew, tipped with beads, and draped down his back all the way to the ground. It should have looked pretentious or like an affectation, but Kwaskwi wore it with all the confidence and ease of a King born to his role—a powerful male surveying his kingdom.

Then he flashed his trademark big-toothed grin, sweeping his arms to the side in a bow straight out of a BBC historical. "Portland welcomes you," he said, breaking the awestruck silence. "The Council honors the Portland Kind as we mourn the passing of Dzunukwa Assu Laich-kwil-tach tonight." I'd never heard Dzunukwa's full name before, part of the cautionary nature of Kind against the dangerous power of true names. Apparently, that changed if the person was dead.

People were crowding closer, leaving the tent unoccupied except for Burly Guy. Kwaskwi was making this into political spectacle, a move I expected but that still made me both nervous and angry. From the sharpened cast of Ken's cheekbones and the warrior-ready stance, he was a bit uncomfortable, too. Pon-suma gave a slow nod. Ken stalked forward.

"I am Ken Fujiwara," he said, bowing in general to the clumps of assembled people. "Lately of the Council but beholden to them no longer."

A flurry of gasps and muffled exclamations rippled through the crowd. Burly Guy and Table Lady looked flabbergasted. Neither of them stood down from alert, ready-to-rumble postures. They must have recognized Ken's name as that of the Council's assassin, the Bringer. Bringer-of-Death.

Ken circled back to where Marlin and I stood. He knelt on one knee.

I gaped at him, appalled.

"Now I am pledged to the Baku Herai Koi."

Bastard. At least he didn't use my full real name here like he did at the Council, but still he was throwing me under the spectacle bus.

Kwaskwi glared at Ken as if he'd just stolen the last French fry from Kwaskwi's plate. *Don't like being upstaged, do we?*

"She's the Council's?" I heard Table Lady exclaim. She stepped backwards when she realized I noticed her comment, as if expecting me to go Incredible Hulk and lunge over the table for her throat. Was it my connection to the Council that caused the reaction, or that I was a Baku?

Kwaskwi's grin stretched to show more teeth than a horse. He prowled over in a showy imitation of Ken's feral walk to complete our tableau. Standing between us, he rested one hand on my shoulder and another on Ken's. "Roll with this," he hissed without moving his lips. Then, in a voice loud enough to reach the entire plateau, "Koi joins us tonight as a recognized Hafu, a protected member of the Portland Kind."

"What did you just do?" I didn't whisper.

"Gave you my protection," said Kwaskwi.

"Claimed you away from the Council," Pon-suma added drily.

"Made you bound by debt and family tie to settle this murder," said Ken. Hairs rose on the backs of my wrists and neck at the threatening rasp of his voice.

"Marlin, too," I said to Kwaskwi, urgently. Whatever officially becoming part of the Portland Kind meant, whatever protection they could afford, I wanted it for my sister.

Kwaskwi's nostrils flared wide, the only sign that this wasn't going exactly according to plan. "You are sure? This can't be easily undone."

"Yeah, hey," said Marlin. "I didn't agree to this."

"Technically I didn't either," I said. "But I'm not doing this without you. You're as Hafu as I am."

The wide smile finally reached Kwaskwi's eyes, crinkling them at the corners. Two Herai and an ex-Bringer Assassin joining the Portland Kind in one night when Dad had refused to be a part of it for so long. This was a coup. "And her sister Herai Marlin," his voice boomed.

Those around us were as rattled by this series of announcements as I was. No one seemed to know if they should be cheering or running away screaming. Kwaskwi gave an infinitesimal jerk of his chin in Burly's direction and Burly started a slow-clap that soon caught fire with the rest of the crowd. Table Lady shouted "welcome" and returned to her station, a sign for everyone to swarm the tent for refills and loud chatter. Kwaskwi herded us over to the table, Ken trailing after brushing pine needles from his knee.

"May I present Herai Koi," said Kwaskwi to Table Lady. "This is Marigold Fischer."

Marigold wrote my name on a sticker nametag and handed it over. I stifled a snort. As if anyone here would forget who and what I was. "You're not at all what I expected," she said. "Elise described you as far less…flamboyant."

I bet she did. Especially since Elise first stalked me at Portland Community College before I even knew what I truly was. Before

Ken. Before I dreamed the dreams of dragons. I straightened my posture.

"Where is your daughter?" said Kwaskwi. "I need her as a witness."

Daughter. This was Elise's mother then. Human or Kobold? I peered at Marigold a bit more sharply than was polite. Her dark brown hair, glinting here and there with strands of silver, was pulled back in a severe bun. Her determined chin was slightly raised, and her eyes were the same devastatingly vibrant blue cheerleader shade as Elise. I sucked at telling Kind from human, apparently. I was clueless. Marigold reached for my hand, glossing over my automatic flinch. But Ken's gift of gloves meant that I let her sandwich my palm between the unaccustomed warmth of her hands—a novel sensation. "You'll help find the scum who did this to my Elise?"

I wanted so badly to answer the fierce love in those cheerleader eyes. Dzunukwa, George, Henry, and Elise. They were family now. Kwaskwi knew damn well how deeply claiming me as part of the Portland Kind would reach into my heart. If he asked me now to force a fragment from some cringing human like Brian from the Witch's Castle, I wouldn't be able to say no.

Pete and his Nordvast Uffheim friends better watch out.

This sensation, being surrounded by my tribe, clasping the hand of someone who would accept me despite, or even because, of my freakiness is what I yearned for. *Kwaskwi read me like a book.*

"Yes," I said firmly. Beside me, Ken made a clucking sound with his tongue. Marlin shifted, uncomfortable with her connection to Pete and the attacks, probably. "I will help Kwaskwi." I could find more for him to go on then just Pete's name and a bunch of tattoos, especially if George or Henry had seen something helpful like a license plate number. Or if I got my hands on Pete again.

"Thank you," said Marigold. She greeted Marlin with the same hand clasp, but did the regal nodding thing with Pon-suma and Ken. "Well, go on to the tent then," she said with a little shooing wave.

"Kwaskwi will need to introduce you to the others." She speared Kwaskwi with a look. "I'll bring Elise over to you when she gets here, but don't you tire her out. She's still mending."

And then somehow we were in the tent and I was being introduced to person after person, their names and faces melting into a huge pot of awkward mishmash. I just couldn't keep up. Five minutes into the greeting process my lips ached in a desperate smile. I shot a panicked glance at Marlin.

She sidled up closer and took over the majority of polite chit chat. Kwaskwi granted her a calculating glance, as if it had never occurred to him how useful she could be. He went back and forth between me and where Pon-suma and Ken were caught in their own little whirlpool of people eager to press the flesh of Council envoys. Every other person asked me about Dad or Ken. Their reputations vied with each other for craziest stories. Most of the Kind knew Dad had lived here, but since he and Kwaskwi had made a pact about keeping everyone away from the Baku's family, no one knew what Marlin and I were capable of, really.

"Had enough?" Kwaskwi came up and squeezed me in a one-armed hug, the tips of the feathers on his Bonnet tickling my cheek and eyes.

"She's about to hit maximum overload," said Marlin.

"Just one more," said Kwaskwi raising his hand in the air. "To avoid nuclear Koi meltdown."

Burly guy left his sentry position and lumbered over. His long, full beard brushed the top of a muddy brown Carhartt jacket. He held out the hairiest knuckled hand I'd ever seen, making my own hand look ludicrously small but his handshake was gentle and cautious, as if my hand were a baby bird. "I'm Kolyma," he said in a voice that rumbled at the same low octave as James Earl Jones.

"Kolyma needs to imprint your scent," said Kwaskwi matter-of-factly as if that needed no further explanation.

"What are you?" The question slipped out before my overloaded social filter could engage. Ken had told me it was rude to ask straight out, but everyone here knew exactly what I was. It was unfair that I was clueless.

Kolyma didn't seem to mind. "I'm a Bear Brother." *Like Henry and George.*

Something smoky and bitter thickened my throat. I curled fingernails into my palms.

"Bear Brother is a Kind name, like Kitsune or Crow or Kobold," said Kwaskwi. "We are all family but George and Henry are Kwakwąką'wakw. Kolyma is Odul. From arctic Siberia."

That distinction didn't help any of the physical sensations telling me I should be ashamed that I played a part in this man's brothers being attacked by Nazis gunning for me.

"Okay folks, that's enough," Kwaskwi said to those still milling around. "We've got business to attend to."

Slowly, people set down their stemware and started filing out from under the tent, led by Kwaskwi. Someone tapped me on the shoulder.

Another Bear Brother, a line of stitches at his scalp and sporting bruised eyes and an arm in a sling, stood mournfully by. I looked up into the huge, dark eyes, pupils so wide barely any white showed. *George. This is George.*

Kwaskwi hovered, a worried frown on his face. "This isn't the best time to tell her."

"Tell me what?"

Kwaskwi sighed and folded his arms across his chest, bracing himself. "Henry suffered internal injuries."

"Henry? But he's okay, right? *Right?*"

George shook his head and put a fist to his heart, thumping it sharply several times. His shoulders shook silently. A tear welled up in his left eye, trailing down his cheek to his nose and settled there, gleaming wetly.

Gone. Henry is gone? I couldn't process that information. My mind refused to understand I would never ride in the Subaru again ignoring his over-explanatory chatter, or experience his snuffly good cheer. *Who will speak for George now?*

I heard Ken explaining to Marlin about the Bear Brothers, but I was gripped by the unfamiliar urge to wrap my arms around George, as if that would be comforting. As if that would make up for failing to have helped in the first place way back at Witch's Castle. Sour regret rose in the back of my throat. "I'm so sorry, George. I'm so sorry."

George tilted his head back, his hands curling into claws and roared.

CHAPTER EIGHTEEN

The sound shook the tent poles and made my teeth ache with its resonance of devastation and loss. Instantly, Kolyma returned, circling George with both arms and squeezing him tight. Kolyma's jacket sleeve rode up, exposing a metal prosthetic arm. George buried his face in the other Bear's shoulder, his body racked with sobs. In the vacuum created by the cessation of that roar, Kwaskwi swiftly flew to the altar, lit a torch, and by the force of his charisma, commanded the eyes of all assembled without a word.

He spread his arms wide. From the top of every tree ringing the plateau a jay rocketed into the night sky with a skull-splitting cacophony of cries. As they faded away, Marigold did something that turned off the fairy lights. A chill darkness wrapped us in smothering weight. We all instinctively shuffled closer to the altar and the only source of warmth: the torch in Kwaskwi's hand.

"We remember Dzunukwa Assu Laich-kwil-tach. We mourn the loss of Henry Gala Wakashan," he intoned. Gasps arose from the crowd. This was the most over-staged bit of obvious manipulation I'd encountered with the Kind since the Council's Kawano and the Eight

Span Mirror's Murase had a verbal dogfight a few days ago, but somehow, against my will and morbanoid sense of irony, Kwaskwi's words hit with the cold shock of an ice water shower. A bitter aching knot spread from under my ribs into my arms, making my fingers numb and cold inside my gloves.

He had us all under his spell. Marlin's eyes were huge, reflecting the fiery glow of the torch. Her lips were parted slightly.

"But this night is not reserved solely for mourning." Another torch flared into life behind Kwaskwi, the warm yellow turning the bearer's hair into a crown of dark gold. Elise.

She was beautiful even with the ugly bruises on her neck visible in the flickering light, the very opposite of a cowed victim. Something excited and giddy shone from her eyes, despite her upper lip curled almost in a sneer. As if part of her hungered for more than the assembled crowd.

I blinked, and that *something* was gone, and Elise was a wholesome cheerleader again.

Kwaskwi continued. "We celebrate life as well. For as our family looses two spirits on their Round Dance to the Sky, the loss is balanced by the renewed gift of Elise's life." Kwaskwi settled his hands on her shoulders, a benevolent father. "We are enriched by the Hafu in our Portland circle. They are our children, our mortal dream of the future." He lifted a fist in the air. "They make us strong!"

A chorus of answering cries came from the crowd. The surging excitement was palpable, heady stuff. George lifted his head from Kolyma's shoulder, both men began thwacking their chest with a rhythmic fist. Elise's name was called out, as well as the names of others I'd probably met this night. She preened and poised like a Beauty Pageant contestant, waving to individuals with a regal dignity. This was more a high school pep rally than a funeral. While one part of me observed how skillfully Kwaskwi was playing the crowd, another, deeper part of me yearned to join in wholeheartedly, to feel the grief unabashedly and the prideful fervor of Kolyma and

Marigold unrestrained by self-consciousness and cynicism.

Kwaskwi lifted his arms again like a mad organist in a gothic movie. The eagle feathers on his bonnet rippled in an invisible wind. The crowd went quiet. "The Pacific Basin Kind enter a new era. The Council in Tokyo is in shambles," he intoned. Pon-suma grimaced, and Ken arched an eyebrow.

"Their insistence on purity has blinded them to what the modern world requires: Kind who are both of our most ancient lineages and also able to move purposefully in the human world. Portland, San Francisco, Honolulu have a chance. A chance to show the entire Pacific Basin where the future lies."

Marigold approached the altar with a tray covered with an embroidered cloth. She nodded to Kwaskwi and Elise. Kwaskwi swiped the cloth away revealing an Olympic Torch. Lifting it from Marigold's tray, he held it up to the crowd. "So let the Hafu take precedence. Let one who is both strong and naïve, ancient and new, bid farewell to Dzunukwa tonight to mark this new future for Portland." He did something to the bottom of the torch and it flared to life, the flames a gorgeous palette of deep reds, oranges, and at the heart the deepest blue.

Elise half-turned towards Kwaskwi, nodding her head with a self-satisfied smile.

But Kwaskwi was looking out over the crowd, searching for a face. Ken gave a short, harsh exclamation in my direction. "*Ganbare!*"

Why is he wishing me *good luck?* And then the crowd was clapping and cheering. A path opened up between me and the altar. Marlin pushed me from behind. "Go on!" she said. "He's calling for you."

Panic froze me. Too many eyes, too many expectations and too little understanding of what was going on left me limp like a stringless marionette. "Herai Koi, let me escort you," said Ken in English, suddenly by my side. With gently applied pressure, Ken walked me down the social gauntlet. He murmured a litany of soothing phrases in my ear. I reached the altar, and Kwaskwi muttered under his breath. "Deer in headlights."

Ken countered with "What did you expect?"

Elise gave a scoff followed by a piercing look of disapproval but moved grudgingly to the side.

"Koi Herai, of the ancient Herai Baku lineage, accept this torch. Light the pyre of our murdered sister, Dzunukwa, and send her soul on its dance to the sky."

I stifled an inappropriate giggle. He was serious. Kwaskwi wanted me to play Hafu poster child. *What is his game plan?*

Kwaskwi thrust the torch into my hands. "Play along like a good little Baku, Koi, you owe me this."

I'd never even seen a funeral pyre before. What did one do? I shuddered. A long bundle of cloth the length and size of a body lay atop bundles of twigs tied with twine, all stacked on top of bigger branches and logs. Dzunukwa's body looked so small versus the fearful memory of her looming over me with her icy, breath-stealing cries back at Pioneer Square. The smell of kerosene stung my nose. I leaned over and put the torch against the nearest bundle of twigs. They glowed a little orange, but didn't catch. "Ken," Kwaskwi stage whispered, "if you would. We need more theatricality."

Ken closed his eyes, the tiny muscles around his mouth tightening. His hands curled into fists at his side. The blue heart-flame of the torch leapt onto the funeral pyre. A wail went up from the crowd as dancing fire engulfed Dzunukwa's pyre. At first, the air was still cold, the pyre alight with Ken's illusion. Then Kwaskwi grasped my arm and made a little flinging motion, releasing the torch into the middle of the pyre. A blast of real heat flushed my face. From the heart of the dancing blue flames an orange-red conflagration unfurled like a giant, fiery rose. Again, George let out a roar, this time joined by Kolyma as well as others scattered across the crowd.

Kwaskwi's expression was solemn, but this close, I could see glints of delight dancing in his eyes. He reached back and tugged a feather free from his Bonnet and dropped it into the pyre.

This was full blown melodrama. The level of emotion thickening the air, the sting of kerosene and ash inside my nose, and the conflicting sensations of cold night air on my neck and the heat of Dzunukwa's pyre on my face—overwhelming. A part of me, buried deep inside under emotional sedimentary rock accumulated from years of shutting myself off from people, awoke. It broke through its rock prison and stretched. This part of me, not Survivalist, not Morbanoid, was as pleased by the crowd's attention as Elise. I bit my lip. It would be easy to allow Kwaskwi's manipulation to mess with my ego.

But Survivalist Koi was sending out urgent flight signals. This didn't feel altogether…right. Kwaskwi was forcing me into a role I wasn't prepared to play. I wasn't sure I could be the emotional focus for all these people. The shivers returned full force. I couldn't stop my teeth from chattering.

"Are you okay?" said Ken. He gripped my arm. I was so shaky he was taking most of my weight.

Marigold returned without her tray. She began singing the famous chorus from that Leonard Cohen song—Hallelujah—celebrating the painful sacredness of brokenness and death. The entire crowd joined Marigold in the chorus: Kwaskwi in a pleasantly rumbly basso and Elise in a thready soprano. The snap and crackle of the fire made a rhythmic counterpoint. This song never failed to tug on my heart strings, even when I was watching K. D. Lang's YouTube cover. Under the velvet sky of a million stars with a crowd of people singing together, their faces illuminated by dancing flames—it crushed my heart into little pieces. Survivalist Koi could shut the hell up. I inhaled smoky air. Being here, amongst these people and sharing their grief, was the genuine belonging I'd longed for my whole life.

A crack of thunder, closer than it possibly could be in the cloudless sky overhead, startled me out of my maudlin miasma. No one else flinched.

Thunder crashed again. Electrical awareness, the ebb of air pressure flowing out before a storm, saturated the plateau. Marigold and Kwaskwi lifted their faces to the starry sky, palms upraised like holy rollers.

A single, brilliant flash of jagged lightning whip-cracked down from the sky and struck the pyre with a boom like a car backfiring. The narrow bundle at the heart of the flames glowed intensely gold, and the smell of ozone stung tears from my eyes. I rubbed at them with a fist. As I blinked them clear, there was a brilliant flash of light and the bundle crumbled away into ash. The leaping flames quieted, burning in a with a steady glow.

There was a collective exhale of breath from the assembled crowd. The emotional fury from before settling into a slow simmer. Whispers and muffled conversations murmured from every direction.

From the sky above, a great shadow drifted down on the far side of the pyre to perch on a boulder at the highest tip of the plateau. It was an eagle as big as a compact car, the flickering flames turning his plumage into a manic dance of molten red and gold. He arched his neck and let loose a piercing shriek. The crowd hushed, a few falling to one knee.

Thunderbird.

Slowly, ever so slowly, Thunderbird tilted his great head so that one eye, half-shuttered by a heavy lid, faced me. I'd only seen Thunderbird in the daylight before, and even then, his vibrant eyes had tugged at me. Here, in the dark, that effect was amplified tenfold.

His pupils were lit from within by a brilliant fire. It was as if someone had dropped precious metals into lava and swirled it in mesmerizing patterns. I felt a tug at the center of myself, deep inside my belly where the Baku flame flickered into life in answer to Thunderbird's challenging stare. I took a step forward, reaching out a hand towards the great bird.

Oh you great beauty. Let me touch you.

"Koi!"

I ignored Ken and took another step. A distant part of me noticed a burning heat emanating from the soles of my feet, but the rest of me was consumed with a fierce desire to taste, to feel the power of the dreams surging behind Thunderbird's gorgeous eyes. I tugged at my left glove, desperate for bare flesh.

The next thing I knew Ken was tackling me to the ground as smoke wafted from my sexy boots—now charred. I'd stepped into the pyre.

What is wrong with me?

But even as the question formed in my brain, I looked up at Ken's angry face, already knowing the answer. I was a monster. And the monster in me always hungered for the dreams of other beautiful monsters.

CHAPTER NINETEEN

"Take me home," I said, squeezing my eyes shut. If I didn't see Thunderbird, he couldn't seduce me.

"I've got you," said Ken. I felt his arms go under my legs and back. He scooped me up against his chest, and I snuggled my face into his neck to lessen the temptation to look across the pyre at Thunderbird.

"Leaving so soon?" said Kwaskwi's voice.

"She's done," said Ken. His voice was that steady, controlled rasp that meant he was very, very angry. A tense silence followed—the boys trying to establish dominance with pure force of will. It tempted me to remove my face from Ken's warm salty-smelling skin, but just the thought of facing Thunderbird again made me whimper.

The delicious, golden promise of Thunderbird's dreaming was a siren call. Like the dragons Ullikemi and the Black Pearl, his dreams would be so sweet, so powerful, my Baku self would gleefully devour them. Their power would fill me like a swelling water balloon until this fragile, human body of mine burst.

Or worse, until I consumed so much that I tapped into his life energy and extinguished his light forever. I'd almost done that to Dzunukwa, and I *had* done it to Yukiko.

I swatted away the memory of Yukiko splayed out in the tundra of her dreamscape, her white hair lost in the swirling snowflakes, her lips a blood blossom. *Don't go down that path.*

"You pushed her too far already," Ken was saying. "You got your little show."

There was more arguing. It was hard to follow with the siren lure of Thunderbird's gaze caressing my exposed skin in feather light touches of warmth. Marigold and Elise joined in the verbal fray, followed by Marlin's familiar contralto.

"I need a Herai for this next part," said Kwaskwi.

"You need a Hafu," Elise insisted.

"Pon-suma and Ken are too much servants of the Council," Kwaskwi countered in a low voice. "Who else embodies the Portland strength of Hafu in contrast to the Tokyo Council? I need a Herai."

"Not this one," said Ken, growing so rumbly I could feel the vibrations in his chest.

"I'll stay," said Marlin.

There was a chorus of dismayed sounds. "Well," said Kwaskwi, "That might actually be even better."

"You've got to be kidding!" I could just about hear the flounce in Elise's step as she moved away.

"Wait," Kwaskwi commanded as Ken began carrying me away. Ken stopped, going tense. The pressure of Thunderbird's gaze and the crackling of the pyre faded. I lifted my head. Ken had maneuvered the tent between us and the pyre. People milled around, leaving this area mostly deserted. So why did it still feel like all eyes were on me? A prickly feeling lifted baby hair on the nape of my neck.

"Something's—"

"Shh!" Ken commanded. He slowly let my legs slide down to the ground while keeping a tight grasp on my upper body.

From the treetops surrounding the plateau came the angry squawking of jays. They rose into the sky and like miniature kamikaze planes dive bombed the path leading towards the parking lot.

Thunderbird screamed.

A flash of white passed by—a giant wolf—chased by a lumbering grizzly bear.

Pon-suma and George.

Ken waltzed us awkwardly toward the edge of the plateau just as a sound like champagne uncorking reached my ears.

Pop. Pop. Pop. A whole case of bubbly.

"Get down," Ken said, pushing me face-first into the weed-covered rocks at the edge of the plateau. My right hand flopped over the edge sending small stones skittering down into the darkness. I peeked. The cliff face sheared off abruptly, a drop that looked like it was five stories down. I swallowed. There was only one way on or off this plateau unless you had wings—towards the champagne pops.

Gunshots, Survivalist Koi pointed out.

I flinched at another round. Ken's breath came harshly ragged above me.

"Marlin's still out there," I said.

"Stay here." Ken disappeared. Literally. Kitsune illusion blended him into the rocky terrain. Thunder rumbled ominously and I raised myself a couple inches just in time to see three bolts of lightning strike one after another in a straight line along the parking lot path.

More screams now. And growls. Shivers wracked my frame and my teeth chattered so badly I bit my own tongue. With the taste of blood came the smell of smoke. Trees were aflame, exposing the silhouettes of struggling men and Kind. I twisted around, half crawling along the ground, heedless of the sharp bite of nettles and pebbles in the palms of my hands. I had to get back to Marlin. The gunshots stopped.

A gust of wind knocked me back down, turning my hair into a

streaming tangle of knots twisting around my face. Thunderbird sliced through the air, Kwaskwi settled between his great wings, mouth open in a yell that was drowned out by the growing sounds of the fighting.

My heart struggled within my ribcage, terrified for Marlin. I had to get back to the pyre. With the multiple fires darkness no longer shrouded the plateau. I could see Elise standing in front of a broken pile of dying embers, her hand on Marlin's arm as if to restrain her. I pulled myself around the wreckage of the tent, close enough for the expression of paralyzing fear on Marlin's face to register.

And on Elise's, a triumphant expression of glee.

"What are you doing?" Ken was back. He swept me up against his chest again. He smelled of acrid smoke, and where my hand touched his back his jacket was torn and sticky. Pon-suma hovered just beyond, hair no longer the orange-brown of dyed Asian black, but brilliant white except for streaks of dark red and ash. His usually stoic face was set in grim determination, as if every ounce of control was necessary just to be standing there, human.

"Marlin," I managed to say through gritted teeth.

"She's okay. Elise will get her away," Ken said in Japanese.

"No!"

"The attackers are contained. She'll be fine."

"Not Elise."

Ken looked down at me, face gone feral and sharp-planed but for the startled narrow eyes. He must have seen the determination in my expression. "Pon-suma!" he said, followed by a string of commands in incomprehensibly growled yakuza slang-laden language.

Pon-suma gave himself a little shake, loosening muscles in his shoulders and long arms. He deliberately caught my eye and put a closed fist to his chest, only to fling it away with an open palm unmistakably in my direction. "By the gate," he said, and then he streaked toward the pyre, the only figure moving with purpose amongst the terrified, crouching Kind who were not part of the melee on the parking lot path.

Another lone pop brought on a chorus of fearful cries.

Lightning struck again, an explosion of heat and light that stung my cheeks and forced my eyes closed. I rubbed away gummy tears to the heart-clenching sight of Thunderbird descending to the ground over leaping flames in a rush of smoke-choked air and flapping wings.

"This is our chance," said Ken. He made a break for the edge of the plateau again, skirting the sheer drop-off close enough to make my stomach tighten. We headed toward the path, now obscured by billowing clouds of smoke and ash stirred up by Thunderbird's slowly stroking wings.

"Wait. Marlin!"

"They're right behind us," said Ken. He tightened his arms around me and pressed a kiss to my forehead, his lips warm. "Just trust me, Koi-chan," he whispered in Japanese against my skin. "Stay quiet."

We disappeared. One moment Ken's dark-on-dark eyes were boring intense holes into me, and the next all I could see was the dark outline of tree canopy. He was using illusion to make us all but invisible. The general clamor had quieted down and as we neared the top of the path where Thunderbird stood sentry, the smoke thinned.

A row of men dressed in camouflage and ski masks knelt in the carpet of pine needles with hands clasped behind their necks. Utility or ammo belts and some kind of paramilitary gear were heaped in piles along with thick pointy guns that were probably semi-automatic or something similarly awful. A smaller pile of cell phones and a video camera lay at the feet of Kwaskwi, terrifyingly fierce in his pristine regalia and a grin that showed all his big teeth.

Along the tree line, a black bear and polar bear sat on their haunches with backs against tree trunks keeping vigilant watch. A handful of men and women still in their formal finery, now ripped and stained with various body fluids, examined each other's wounds. Two or three of the Kind were as short as adolescents, but their presence here and wrinkled faces marked them adult. One of them was Marigold, watching the prisoners with long, wickedly barbed knives gripped in both hands. No one was lying motionless on the ground, thankfully. No one was dead.

We wouldn't kill them, right?

Kwaskwi loped down the row emanating menace and power. A few of them visibly flinched as he drew near. A kneeling man let loose a muffled sob. Kwaskwi zeroed in on him, third from the end. He stood in front of the guy, hands on his hips, as Ken carried me past Thunderbird. I shut my eyes tight against the danger of the ancient eagle's eyes and opened them again just in time to find Marigold peering in our direction in a way that left no doubt she could see us.

Kobolds aren't fooled by illusion. It was something to file away in my growing pile of unorganized facts about Kind. Ken stopped our forward progress as Kwaskwi pulled the guy up by the collar of his bulky camo jacket and strode over to the edge of the cliff. With two straight arms he held the guy over the edge, shoulder muscles bunched with effort.

"Marigold," Kwaskwi commanded. She went to another kneeling man and worked the tip of a knife underneath his ski mask.

"They can't," I whispered to Ken. He stopped but squeezed his arms around me in warning.

Marigold pulled the guy up to a stand, slicing through his mask at the same time. Familiar golden Thor features emerged. It was Pete. From the clear space behind us came a feminine gasp. *Marlin.* She and Pon-suma were invisible to me like we were to them.

"How many more are there out in the forest?" Kwaskwi's question was directed at the sobbing man hanging mid-air, but it was Pete who answered.

"No one," said Pete.

Kwaskwi released one hand from his dangling guy. Immediately the guy dropped three feet so that his head was parallel with the cliff edge. "How many? You wouldn't attack with a half-dozen men."

"I didn't know, I swear!" The dangler was sobbing, almost incoherent. "They called you demons...but I thought that was just...I didn't know you were *monsters*."

All the kneeling men turned to face the cliff, arms lowering. The bears and Marigold allowed it.

Thunderbird rustled his wings. Three of the kneeling guys scrambled backwards.

Pete didn't seem fazed. He smiled into Marigold's knife, hovering close to his face. "We didn't know about your *pet*."

Marigold leaned in closer. "Thunderbird is not a pet."

Kwaskwi clucked his tongue against his teeth. "Let me do the talking. Dammit, my arm is getting tired. Who's left in the woods?"

Dangling man's hands scrabbled at rocks and loose dandelions, sobbing uncontrollably what sounded like male first names.

"Shut up!" Pete said. "I am your Grand Dragon. I order you to shut up."

Kwaskwi sighed and dragged the dangler up onto the edge. The guy lay panting and gasping, squeezing nettles between his fingers like they'd save him from slipping backwards to a painful death on the stones below.

Grand Dragon. I released a sobbing breath. Always the dragons causing me problems.

Ken started moving again down the path.

"*Matte*," I said. *Wait. We can't just leave.*

"I can't protect you if they see your face," Ken whispered in my ear. "Do you really want to be part of this?"

The black bear, George, tilted its head to aim an ear in our direction. *Great. Now only the humans were fooled by Ken's illusion.* What would Kwaskwi and Marigold and George think of us running away like this? After welcoming me and Marlin into the Portland Kind. Just when the going got tough.

"I'm already part of this," I said quietly.

"And so am I," said Marlin's whisper behind us. "They already know my face, Ken. Un-invisible me."

"Not a good idea," I said, struggling to get my feet on the ground. Ken maintained an iron grip.

"Get behind George," said Ken. "If you appear suddenly out of thin air it will make things worse."

"Give me a couple seconds," said Marlin.

Thunder rumbled overhead again, but the moon was slipping below the tree line. Behind the looming shadow of Mt. Hood, the sky was losing its deep, velvet black. A grayish pink line marked the horizon. Dawn wasn't too far away.

Kwaskwi joined Marigold in front of Pete. "You will answer my questions now. Or I will feed you to my friend."

"You wouldn't dare hurt me. How you gonna explain dead bodies to the police?"

Kwaskwi grinned. "No evidence left if you're bear food."

Marlin stepped out from behind George. She came to stand over Pete, looking down at him with the scarily bland expression Dad used on busboys who left grains of rice on the bamboo sushi mats after cleanup. "I'm not afraid of the police," she said, and tensed her leg.

"Bitch," Pete snarled. "All you ching chong sluts are insane."

Marlin hauled off and kicked Pete in the nuggets. "I filed a harassment complaint, asshole. You're not supposed to get within thirty feet of me. You run snotfaced to the police. I dare you."

He yowled like a tomcat, doubling over and rocking in pain. Kwaskwi grinned. A handful of chattering jays emerged from the tree line and buzzed around Kwaskwi's head, perching fitfully on George's shoulders. He gave them a rumbled warning, and they settled, turning beady eyes onto the kneeling men who stared in open-jawed astonishment underneath their ski masks.

Kwaskwi knelt in front of the first man and pulled off his mask. When the guy tried to cover his face with his hands, Kwaskwi easily pried them away, staring into terrified eyes. He licked his lips. "I have memorized your face." He jerked his chin towards the bears. "The

Bear knows your scent. If you ever show up again, my friends will track you to your houses. We will come in the dead of night, and we will take your wives and girlfriends and daughters and feed them to my hungry friends."

The man's lip trembled. He started chanting the Lord's Prayer. Kwaskwi burst out laughing.

He went down the line, removing the masks from all the men. He slipped a cell phone out of an inside pocket of his jacket. He snapped pictures of each guy. "If I hear one hint of giant eagles or bears or anything at all about us in the news, I will send these photos to the police along with several eye-witnesses from tonight about how your hate group interrupted an important Native American ritual." He grinned slowly. "That's a hate crime, a federal offense. The FBI will do worse than kick you in the balls. And then we'll still come in the night and take your daughters."

"He's bluffing. He won't do any of that. They're spineless demons, sinning hell-spawn. Filth." Pete had recovered his breath. "They're not going to risk the Feds' attention."

Marigold stowed one of her knives in a sheath at the small of her back and held out a hand. With the tip of her other knife she slowly cut a welling line of crimson along her palm. Wetting the tip of her knife with her own blood, she traced concentric circles around Pete's eyes and slashes on his cheeks. Pete grinned, defiant and angry.

Blood. The crazy professor who attacked me when this whole Baku craziness started, Hayk, had cut my cheek to fuel mind control magic. Kind magic required a release of life energy, either birth or death, or blood. It struck me for the first time that Baku had a third path to acquiring life energy—eating dreams.

Marigold closed her eyes, saying something harsh in a Germanic sounding language. Pete reached for the crucifix around his neck and held it out in a warding motion like she was a vampire.

"Stupid asshole," said Marlin.

The places where blood streaked Pete's face burst into blue flame.

Pete screamed, falling on his face in the pine needles and dirt, batting at the acid flames with his hands.

"Oh shit," said Marlin, inching away from Marigold in horror.

Illusion? No. That was blood magic. Pete's flesh truly burned for agonizing seconds, until the dirt quenched the flames. Marigold let out a sigh, as if pleased by her handiwork, and went to flank Kwaskwi like a loyal lieutenant.

Pete sat up, eyes weeping dirty tears, angry red welts and white blisters decorating the exact patterns where the fire had marked him.

Pon-suma's voice whispered behind us. "I'm staying. You go ahead." I felt Ken tense and a moment later Pon-suma appeared next to Marigold. Kwaskwi, flanked by Pon-suma and Marigold, was horrifyingly magnetic and visceral and undeniably real. A beautiful nightmare come to life. I felt sick to my stomach.

Kwaskwi spared Pon-suma a surprised glance and then drew himself up to his full height, thrusting out his chest. "You have ten minutes to take this pile of shit Grand Dragon of yours and get your sorry asses out of Lewis and Clark. You will never come back." He paused, allowing the power and threat of this statement to sink in. No one moved. Pete glared hatred through the grotesque mask of his wounded face. Kwaskwi made a disappointed cluck and then started counting out loud.

George rose up on his haunches, shaking off disgruntled jays. He roared. Immediately two guys popped up from their kneeling positions, ran to Pete, and dragged him to his feet. Between them, they half-carried Pete in a loping jog down the path, followed closely by the others.

Kwaskwi stopped counting with a grim press of his lips. There were soot-deepened crow's feet at the corners of his eyes, and the mocking glint had disappeared, shading him tired and grey. He jerked a thumb towards the disappearing attackers. George and Kolyma lumbered down the path at a misleadingly sleepy pace. No one was fooled. They would ensure any stragglers were truly gone.

The Kind who hadn't retreated back to the pyre or the tent waited expectantly, entirely focused on Kwaskwi. He bent his head, then slipped off the war Bonnet, reached out to Pon-suma, and pressed his forehead to the quiet man's for a couple of deep breaths. When he turned to grasp the nearest person's arm and speak quietly and urgently, working his way around the gathered circle, there was no sign of grief. His expression was as wild and hard as the hatred I'd seen in Pete's eyes.

CHAPTER TWENTY

Ken made us reappear there in the middle of the leftover partygoers, Marlin staggered over, and we made brief goodbyes to Kwaskwi. He gripped my shoulder in a painfully strong farewell and gave me a skeletal, sparkless version of his usual grin. Ken promised we would meet up after everyone had a chance to catch some sleep.

Considering all the cleanup—the pyre, Thunderbird, the tent, and emotional damage control for the rest of the Kind, I didn't think that would be until late afternoon at the earliest.

Marlin gave no reaction when Ken revealed he had the keys to Pon-suma's Karmann Ghia in his back pocket. We rode together in the back—me slumped over and listless, feeling like a mass of overcooked Sapporo Ichiban noodles, and Marlin stiff and avoiding eye contact. She answered only in monosyllables until Ken pulled us over to the curb in front of the Heathman.

Keith the friendly doorman opened the door and helped Marlin out, but even he didn't get more than a brief nod out of her. Ken drove off to find parking, leaving me to trail Marlin into the lobby. She stopped abruptly at the round settee and sat down on the quilted seat, covering her mouth with the back of her hand.

"Marlin?" I sat next to her.

A wracking sob shook her, and then a choked, gargling sound like she was swallowing back sick. "I can't. This is...I just can't." Her hand muffled the words.

"The funeral is over," I said. "You don't have to go back there."

"I just want to go home."

I closed my eyes, scrounging for something inspiring or at least calming to say. I'd only seen Marlin reach breaking point once before, when Dad was brought home by the police one night during a dementia episode about a week before mom died in the hospital. Then, like now, I was helpless. My sister was happiest when she was in control and had a grasp on all the details of what was going on. I'd been faking it my whole life, so this slide into Kind crazy-town didn't hit me the same way.

"That's not a good idea," I said softly. "It's not safe—"

"Staying with you isn't safe! They were shooting at us. With guns!"

"*Nihongo hanashimasho*," I suggested we speak Japanese in a gentler tone than the urgency I felt required. The early morning hotel patrons stared at us. None of them set off my Japan-dar, luckily.

Marlin switched to Japanese, but not the Herai dialect Dad had taught us, as if she wanted to distance herself from anything related to Dad's background, the Kind...me. "This is fucked up, Koi. At first it was kind of cool, amazing even. Like movies come to life. I was so upset by what Pete had done to me. I needed the distraction. But tonight, that was wrong. She burned Pete's face! And what the hell was that giant eagle?"

I still had on my gloves, smoky with soot and streaked with unmentionable fluids, so I gripped both her hands. "We're alive. We're here." *Pathetic words. Why can't I be more eloquent?* Marlin teetered on the edge of a complete breakdown.

"Yeah, well, I don't want any part of this. I'm going to call the police and make a report against Pete, and then I'm going home. It's what I should have done before."

"I can't protect you if you—"

"I wouldn't need protection if you hadn't gotten us mixed up in this monster stuff in the first place!"

Her words poured a bucket of ice water over my head. This is what she thought—I chose the Kind over her? She didn't understand at all. Not if she thought I skated this close to monsters by choice.

"Low blow," I said, throat constricting.

But Marlin was surfing the resentment crest of her hissy fit. "You promised me you'd get your life together this term. Have you actually stepped foot on the PCC campus this month? I bet you aren't answering gig emails from the Portland Perlmongers, either."

My cheeks flushed. I was completely ignoring email these days but her accusations were still unfair. Marlin pulled out of my grip. "You think playing Kwaskwi's golden girl is the kind of life you want? Shooters and beatings and murder?"

"I didn't ask for this," I said. "Take your complaints to Dad."

"Yeah, since you dragged him to Tokyo, he hasn't been in any condition to hold a conversation," Marlin said.

"That's not my fault!"

"Still shirking responsibility, aren't you? All my life I've treated you with kid gloves because you were so fragile, so special. To hell with it. It's time you stepped up for yourself."

"That's what I'm doing."

"So why are white supremacists invading *my* life and trying to shoot *me*? Huh? Why am I suffering the consequences of your decisions?"

I hesitated too long, staring at her. Little spots of pink appeared high on her cheeks. Her eyes widened, challenging me for an explanation. But I couldn't come up with the flimsiest excuse. I didn't ask to be Baku, but every step that brought us here was one I took. She was right.

Marlin blew a scoffing raspberry. "That's what I thought. Well, Koi-chan," she said, making my name drip with scorn, "I'm out. You won't have little sister to lean on. I'm going straight to Cedar Sinai and getting Dad. I'm going to admit him to the Providence Brain and Spine Institute. He needs MRI's and IV's and expert medical care. He doesn't need giant eagles and gunfire."

"I've still got next term's tuition in my account, I can help with the cost."

"Don't bother," Marlin said. "I know I can't go home, but I don't think I can see you for a while. I'll find my own place to stay and keep you updated on Dad's progress at Providence, but don't call or text me back. We need some time to figure out how I'm going to fit into your new life."

"Marlin."

"No ginger," she said. "There's just no ginger for this situation." She stood up from the settee. "Figure this all out, Koi," she added in English. "And don't take too long." She closed her eyes, shaking her head. Her next breath caught in her chest. Then she turned on her heel and barreled out the Heathman's front doors.

My sister left me. And she was taking Dad with her. All my life— through Dad leaving us and Mom's death—Marlin had been the one constant. Without her it was like being lost back in the shadowed, heavy canopy forest of Broughton Bluffs, without even the moon or the stars to show the path home.

Ken found me ten minutes later, still sitting there, tears silently dribbling down my face. He sat on the opposite side of the settee so his back was to me, giving me space to pull myself together. After a few sniffling moments, he handed over a small packet of tissues emblazoned with the heavily made up face of a girl advertising a Shinjuku Hostess Bar. I crumpled it in my hand, unable to look at the girl or the reminder of all the things I'd done in Japan. Running home wasn't an escape from the Baku stuff or the Council, not really.

"Koi?" Ken said after a moment. "Wouldn't you be more

comfortable in the room?"

"Probably," I said. "But apparently I'm such a mess I can't keep from falling apart in public."

Ken stood up and came around to my side of the settee. "That's self-pity talking. Come on, Koi. Let's go to the room." His tone softened. "I promise there'll be chocolate."

I let him pull me up and guide me to the elevator with his hand at the small of my back. It would be so easy to latch onto Ken. I could feel the tidal pull of wanting to lean into him, feel his *kinako* breath on my face, his strong arms around me, and those elegant, long-fingered hands on my cheek. But Ken wasn't the same kind of rock as Marlin. He'd proved that in Tokyo when he'd given the Council my full name and kept me in the dark about his true loyalty. As if he couldn't quite trust me to play in the adult sandbox.

We entered the room, and I kicked off those stupid boots, and let my sore toes sink into the plush carpet. Still in my smoky clothes, I threw myself across the bed and turned on my side away from Ken. Since stepping foot in Portland he'd returned to being the Ken I'd gotten to know first. The Ken who followed me to a crazy murdering Professor's office at PCC and trusted me to make a deal with Kwaskwi. Never smothering me with advice or manipulating me with his feelings, only going feral Kitsune when my loved ones were in danger. Like tonight.

Which was he, really? The inscrutable century old arrogant Council servant? Or the man who sat on my kitchen stool and devoured overcooked spaghetti with burnt sauce just to make me comfortable?

Expecting him to be some kind of perfect white knight was crazy. So what he'd lived longer than Betty White or Methuselah. Not every octogenarian was a sage. Long life didn't necessarily make you wiser, it just gave you more time to fuck things up. I turned over on my back and found Ken standing at the foot of the bed, his arms crossed at his chest. As the moment held, he slowly arched an eyebrow—a question, a challenge. I didn't know if I had it in me to answer.

Maybe...maybe whirlwind true love romance like the books and the movies and all that wasn't something for me. Maybe this was my chance for the closest thing possible I could find—two broken people willing to share the jagged pieces of themselves with each other. Marlin's angry accusations about my irresponsibility played back like a movie soundtrack over images—Dzunukwa's frightened face at Pioneer Square when I'd almost sucked her dry, the human witness, Brian, at the Witch's Hut, and finally Yukiko's lifeless eyes framed by tangled, white hair fading into the endless tundra of her most intimate, dream of herself.

Maybe jagged pieces were all a monster deserved.

"You're too quiet," said Ken. "I'm going to come lie down next to you now." He paused, waiting for permission.

I bit my lower lip and nodded. The bed dipped as he settled his long, muscular body next to mine. He bent his elbows and pillowed his head on his clasped hands. "So...your sister is having trouble with the way things went down tonight."

I nodded again.

"Yeah," he said.

We lay there, breathing, until I couldn't stand not seeing what expression was on his face. *Please, please don't let it be pity.* Or worse, the careful distance of someone unintentionally tangled too deep and on the retreat. I turned my head to find Ken's face hovering very close.

The irises of those dark chocolate eyes had widened again, bleeding into the whites so that Ken regarded me as his feral Kitsune self.

Oh. I couldn't ignore that intensity focused on me. As if I were the last drop of water in a parched desert.

"Know this, Koi AweoAweo Herai Pierce," he said, giving me my whole name, the syllables a physical sensation like the brush of warm fur down my face and chest. "Being Hafu has twisted me my whole life. One foot in Kind politics, one foot in the human world. Rejecting one for the other always ended badly. Until I met you, here in Portland. You are figuring out how to be both in a way I never thought possible. The closer I bind myself to you, the closer I am to knowing who I should be. You are my last chance, my only possible dream of a future."

It was too much. Too much pressure. I had no words to answer his wanting.

Instead, I turned all the way over, arching into him, pressing my lips to the place on his left jaw where his anger tic beat a wild pulse. He groaned, hands coming up to grip my shoulders. I put a hand to his cheek, stubble catching at the soft silk of my glove. Ken hissed at the glove. Intertwining fingers in mine, he slipped his other hand underneath the edge of the glove's sleeve in a soft tickle that raised goose bumps across my upper arm and back.

"You refused my dreaming back in Japan," Ken said softly. "Please, give me another chance."

My left arm was trapped between us, so I put my index finger to my lips, biting the silk tip and easing the glove off. Finger by finger I continued, peeling back the glove and all Survivalist Koi's objections about the danger of vulnerability, both of my skin and my heart.

Somehow, in the craziness of the last few weeks, I'd grown brave. Or maybe my heart was growing calluses. When Marlin used to bake cookies, Mom would steal them straight out of the oven. Her fingertips had been burned so many times she didn't feel it anymore. But no, my heart wasn't tough and insensitive. I was feeling everything, all the way down to my curling toes.

When the glove was off, I tugged at the top buttons of Ken's shirt, pushing it away to reveal the smooth caramel expanse of well-defined pectorals. I placed my naked palm flat on the warm skin, tensing each finger in turn just to watch the heat darken his eyes into the same velvet night as the sky over the plateau.

Ken closed the distance between us, pressing his lips to mine in a soft, urgent question of a kiss. I closed my eyes and chased after the kiss when he started to withdraw. And for once, I let myself fall into him.

No worrying about placement of teeth or where to stroke my tongue. We breathed in each other's breath, lips moving onto jawlines, ears, and sensitive necks. Ken rucked up my dress and his hands burrowed underneath the material to grip my hips, warm and solid and undeniably there, with me, here and now.

And then the world was spinning 360 degrees, and I was in Ken's familiar innermost dream, the essence of himself. I ran through a primeval forest of fragrant *hinoki* cypress with a sense of innocent exhilaration chased by a fierce hunger. Before me, the figure of a woman with long, dark hair, bathed in the silvery brilliance of the moonlight, shone like a beacon. The impossible, beautiful image of Koi Pierce Ken held in his dream—how he saw me. This was true. There was no Kitsune illusion in a dream. Something hooked me underneath my breastbone and pulled taut, tugging me closer and closer to her. She raised arms outstretched in welcome.

CHAPTER TWENTY-ONE

The stupid buzzing wouldn't stop. I turned away and pulled the pillow over my head. Still it continued. "Ken." My voice croaked.

Either the boy had to quiet his phone, or I was going to throw it out the window. "Ken!"

The softly snoring lump swathed in bed sheets next to me moved. There was a grunt.

"Your phone."

Ken sat up instantly alert like one of those ridonculous people who didn't need caffeine or showers or even sunshine in the morning. He stopped the horrific buzzing before it drove me irretrievably bonkers and greeted the caller with a quick "Hai."

Stupid morning people. I reluctantly shoved the pillow so I could see the Warhol Marilyn Monroe wall clock. Damn. No wonder he was alert, it was already noon! Ken rolled off the bed and headed to the bathroom, still nodding and *hai*-ing into the phone. I seized the chance to do a full body stretch across the big bed, waking up my limbs and grimacing as sore calf muscles protested. I'd slept very, very well last night, despite the jet lag, and had no nightmares at all about

144

Broughton Bluffs. I must have been exhausted. A satisfied smile curved my lips. Or Ken acted on my system like melatonin.

Speaking of Ken, he'd better not hog the bathroom too long, my bladder was practically screaming.

I sat up to consider the room service menu on the bed stand. An expensive hotel like the Heathman surely wouldn't serve instant lattes like gas station machines. They must have an actual barista style machine since they catered to so many foreign rich folks. Time to test that theory. I picked up the bedside phone and pushed the room service button. Ken zoomed back into the room. He grabbed the receiver out of my hand and dropped it in the cradle with a loud crash.

"No time for that."

Chivalrously I refrained from physical violence. "I'm not going to operate well without latte."

"I've got Dalip's cousin Aabi meeting us downstairs in ten minutes."

"Who?"

Ken sighed in a way that meant he was disappointed with my inability to focus. "Our taxi driver's cousin. I'm sure the two of you can find a drive-thru espresso shack between here and Elise's."

"Elise?" Dread thickened the lining of my stomach. My face screwed up like a petulant toddler. "Why are we going there?" A sliver of unease pierced the general unhappiness. "Was there another attack?"

"No," said Ken, all serious. "But Kwaskwi is sure that the Nordvast Uffheim aren't done with us yet. He's meeting us there with…a possible lead."

Discretion sure looked better than valor this morning. *Er…this afternoon.* I retreated to the bathroom rather than dig any further into the implications of Kwaskwi *having a lead.* I would find out soon enough.

Tentatively, I replayed last night's events, sifting through my

K. BIRD LINCOLN

emotional reactions to meeting all those Kind and the Nordvast Uffheim's attack. Henry was gone. Lots to chew on, for sure, but last night's mess was less devastating than the image of Marlin's closed off face as she left the hotel. I picked up my cell from the sink, swiped to messaging, and then put the phone back with a sigh.

It was too soon. Anything I did now would just make things worse. Marlin needed time to cool off. I wished she'd texted something, though, I'd have even been grateful for a poop emoji.

It took me longer than ten minutes to splash water on my face, wrangle my hair into a smooth ponytail down my back, and change out of the t-shirt I'd pulled on last night after Ken divested me of the sexy dress. My choices were limited, but I made do with yoga pants, one of Ken's grey t-shirts, and a button-down red plaid shirt I found hanging in the closet.

When I couldn't delay any longer, I found Ken standing by the door in cargo pants and a grey Henley open at the throat, hair moussed into sexy spikes. He was frowning. I gave him a quick kiss on his pouty lower lip as I moved to open the door. Outside the Heathman, it was Keith again. He gave a fist bump to Ken and a disapproving head shake to me.

A silver Toyota Prius with bumper stickers declaring "Keep Portland Beered" and "Pure Punjabi" under a Lyft sign sat at the curb. "That's yours," said Keith. Ken slipped into the front seat next to the driver—presumably Aabi. He was a young man with a closely trimmed beard and moustache and a turban the same silver as his car.

"Your sister's really disappointed in you," Keith said softly as he handed me into the back.

Seriously? Advice on my family life from a man in a Beefeater costume?

"Where to?" said Aabi. He had a stronger British accent than his cousin. And also grooming.

Ken gave him directions to take the Hawthorne Bridge to the Mt. Tabor area as if he were the Portland native, not me. As we crossed, I

146

leaned forward. "There's a Dutch Brothers drive-thru on SE 26th."

"Kwaskwi seemed anxious."

"He's always anxious," I said grumpily. "It won't kill him to wait an extra ten minutes."

"More like twenty minutes with this traffic," said Aabi.

I lasered holes in the back of his turban with my eyes.

We made it to the coffee shack in record time. I rolled down my window and ordered a large mocha, giving the manic pixie barista at the drive-thru my best smile. Once the elixir of life was warming my hands, and the silken Dutch Brothers trademark chocolate was on my tongue, I settled into the back seat.

Ken arched an amused eyebrow, and then started chatting with Aabi about the weather, the Trailblazers, and which restaurants in Portland served the best chutneys and pickled mango. Too soon, Mt. Tabor loomed ahead as we turned into Elise's residential neighborhood.

There was no green Subaru parked in front of the red bungalow. My heart gave a little twinge. Would George still drive for Kwaskwi?

Ken paid Aabi, and we knocked on the front door.

Kwaskwi opened it, releasing the mouth-watering browned butter scent of pancakes and the smoked salt aroma of good bacon that hadn't been burnt to an inedible crisp a la Koi. "We have breakfast," he said proudly.

I ducked under his arm and beelined for the kitchen.

Chet stood in front of Elise's spiffy gas stove, a gingham checked apron on over pajama bottoms covered in pineapples and a Portland Avalanche cap on his messy blonde hair. I was pretty sure the Avalanche was a gay ruby team, and while I appreciated the muscular rugby biceps the apron revealed, I appreciated the stack of silver-dollar sized pancakes he was sliding off a spatula onto a trendy white bistro plate more.

"Mine, all mine," I said, grabbing the plate.

"Good Morning," Chet said brightly, flashing a genuinely friendly smile. *Another morning person. Sheesh.*

It struck me that he had been conspicuously absent from last night's festivities. "You weren't at Broughton Bluffs," I blurted, instead of "Thank you for the pancakes."

"Yeah." His grin turned sheepish. "I'm still in the closet."

Ken reached around from behind me and stole three whole pancakes from my plate and at least half the pile of cooked bacon waiting on the breakfast bar. "Your family and friends don't know you're Kind?"

Chet laughed. "They don't know I'm *gay*. Of course my parents know I'm half-Kobold. Duh. But I don't hang out near Kwaskwi in public functions. Dad would totally figure it out."

I pointed at his cap and helped myself to more bacon. "That doesn't clue them in?"

Kwaskwi sauntered into the kitchen followed by Pon-suma, silent as a ghost. "*Moniyaw* Kind's capacity to ignore the obvious never ceases to amaze me." He swiped Chet's hat and put it on, bill-backwards. "Even Marigold prefers to stay willfully blind. Kobolds are supposed to have an affinity for seeing truth in the darkness. But Chet's parents hardly ever acknowledge me."

"That's my boyfriend's," Chet said pleasantly. "I'm going to need that back."

At Chet's words, Pon-suma stopped playing ghost and joined the little circle standing around the breakfast bar. He took the hat off Kwaskwi's head, and with a quiet intensity, handed it back to Chet. The two exchanged looks that pretty obviously meant "He's all yours" and "You're an *ex* boyfriend." Kwaskwi couldn't have looked more amused. But then he suddenly wasn't. He dropped onto a stool next to me and rested his chin on his palms. "So...about last night."

I regarded the male faces surrounding me. Where was Elise?

"Last night was crazysauce, um, unexpected," I said. "Please tell me those stupid jerks with their guns are all still alive."

"For now," he said. "But I make no promises for the future.

Someone in the Portland Kind told the Nordvast Uffheim about our gathering. That's clear enough to everyone. We can go on the offensive now."

"Yes," said Ken. "But it's not clear what you want from Koi in all this."

"Don't get your panties in a twist, Kitsune. She still owes me a debt, but out of the munificence of my heart I will not ask her to dream eat a human again. I've got a different plan." Kwaskwi paused, nostrils flaring, as if waiting for someone to beg him to elaborate on his genius plan. I snorted and took the latest batch of Chet's pancakes.

When he realized all of us were too busy chewing, Kwaskwi put his palms flat on the breakfast bar and drew himself up to a ramrod straight sitting position. "We'll lure their leader to an isolated place and take a blood price for the deaths of Dzunukwa and Henry."

"Blood price sounds an awful lot like murder," I said.

"Kind law," Pon-suma said.

I narrowed my eyes. "The Nordvast Uffheim are humans. Shouldn't we be presenting evidence to the police about this?"

"Involving the police in Kind business never ends well," Ken muttered.

Kwaskwi made a hang loose sign and made a drinking motion with it. Chet started fiddling with a lovely red Nespresso machine. My ears perked up. *Espresso? Latte? Another one so fast? Kwaskwi really wanted to get on my good side.*

"We work very hard to stay out of the police's radar," he said. "If we were to bring a complaint against the Nordvast Uffheim, there would be forms and court appearances and formal charges. Our complaints would lend weight to the Nordvast's crazy accusations."

"At the very least," Chet added as he lowered the foaming nozzle into a tiny pitcher of milk, "Broughton Bluffs would get more scrutiny."

"We won't kill him...most likely," said Kwaskwi. "But don't

make the mistake of thinking he's done. He knows we won't go to the police. He's counting on our desire for privacy for protection."

"You sound sure of who the leader is," Ken said putting down his fork.

Kwaskwi turned the full brilliance of his aw-shucks grin on me. A piece of bacon was caught in between two of his giant front teeth. "Sure, we know who it is, don't we, Koi? The one who left those messages for you. The one obsessed with dream eaters and death. The Grand Dragon."

"Pete."

"Otherwise known as James Martin Thorvald."

The pancakes I'd eaten suddenly felt like a gluey pile of rocks at the pit of my stomach. If I saw him again the temptation to unleash my Baku hunger on him would be fierce and I don't know if I'd be able to hold back. That man was dirt. He was so full of hate. I desperately didn't want to become like him or for him to be the catalyst that transformed me into a monster.

On the other hand, he wasn't going to give up, his defiance, even after Marigold burned his face, made that clear enough. Every moment he was free somewhere out there in the city made my skin itch. His messages were meant to taunt me into revealing myself. He knew what I was, and he'd called me an abomination. What was it about my Baku-hood that invoked such unreasoning hate? Ken's theory he was aiming for the heaviest hitter made sense only if he didn't know about Thunderbird. After last night he wouldn't think I was the most powerful Kind anymore. I wasn't an ancient one, or even big and hairy like George and Kolyma.

But when I faced ancient ones before it was always me who walked away from the encounter, Survivalist Koi whispered.

"I'm the bait," I said.

"No." Ken stood up, knuckles white with gripping the edge of the bar.

"You think he'll come after me despite what happened last night?

Despite Thunderbird?"

"Oh sweetie," said Kwaskwi, receiving the freshly foamed latte from Chet and presenting it to me with both hands. "I know obsession when I see it. He wants you. And he's not going to stop until he gets you, one way or another."

CHAPTER TWENTY-TWO

Kwaskwi was surprised to hear that Marlin was no longer in the picture. Her enthusiasm last night to be a part of the Kind and stay and help Kwaskwi before the attack had fooled him into thinking she had accepted everything. I explained my sister was off limits and then snuck away to the bathroom to check text, email, and Instagram. I never posted to Instagram, but Marlin usually had some interior design photo going on two or three times a week at least. Nothing had been posted for two weeks. No new texts or messages from her, either.

I'm sorry, I typed. Then biting my lower lip, I erased it. I tried finding some combination of emojis that were apologetic, but the sad smiley face just seemed pathetic and the hearts too generic to convey the complicated set of feelings between us. Even Asian Santa didn't seem up for the challenge. I sighed, retyped *I'm sorry* and sent it before I could second guess myself again.

I waited for two minutes, but finally gave up and put the phone back in my pocket. Outside the bathroom, Ken and Kwaskwi's raised voices were audible. I hesitated in front of a half-open bedroom door.

It felt like an odd invasion of Elise's privacy being here like this. Although Kwaskwi and Chet seemed right at home.

"Koi?" A voice called out from the darkened bedroom. *Elise.*

"Yes?" My hand hovered at the wood door frame.

"Can you come in here for a moment?"

The room was not at all what I'd pictured for her. There was no ornate oversized vanity mirror or frilly lace curtains. Instead, Elise reclined on a giant Danish Modern low bed propped up by pillows. The size of the bed made her into a lost little girl, the bruises on her throat and visible around her collarbones resembling those of a domestic violence victim.

"How are you feeling?"

"Look," said Elise. "I don't want you getting the wrong impression here. We're never going to be buddies."

I started backing out of the room. Maybe I'd misunderstood. "I'll just head back to the boys."

"Wait." It was a command. "Kwaskwi insists on treating me with kid gloves. He won't tell me anything about the plan."

"The plan?"

"Don't be coy, Koi. What's Kwaskwi's plan for getting back at the bastards who did this to me? And then attacked us last night?"

I considered what I knew about Elise. She made me super uneasy. Even back when I knew nothing about Kind, and she was just another student in my Japanese Lit class at PCC, she'd never been exactly friendly. More like a snarky prickly pear. "He wants to lure them into some kind of trap." My toes curled inside my shoes, trying to grip a ground that seismically shifted into dangerous territory. "And he wants me as bait."

"Figures," said Elise. "Kwaskwi can't seem to make a move without you."

Her tone contained a bit more venom than I was used to even from Elise. Were her fangs out because we were alone? I wasn't in the mood to be Elise's punching bag today. She apparently didn't realize

I wasn't the same old close-mouthed hermit from Kaneko-sensei's class. I'd faced dragons. A petulant cheerleader had no power over my feelings.

"Who was that hooded man in your dream?"

Elise blinked. "What?"

"When I ate your dream, there was a hooded man you were afraid of. Someone associated with the guys who jumped you. But the fear I felt in your dream wasn't of the unknown. There was a quality there, a specific fear."

"A specific fear of *attacking* me. Seriously. Just go tell Chet I need my pain meds, will you?"

I turned toward the door to hide my smile. I'd gotten under her skin, and the petty part of me was pleased I'd turned the tables.

Chet was actually in the hall outside Elise's room. He looked surprised when I emerged. "They need you in the kitchen now."

"Thanks."

"Look, I know Elise isn't easy." Chet gave an apologetic smile. He leaned in close, lowering his voice. "You grew up Hafu outside the community. There are Kind that won't give me or Elise the time of day. Imagine being treated that way your whole life and then a Hafu like you showing up—you're like the worst-case Mary Sue possible, not bad looking and super-talented. So powerful even Kwaskwi is tripping over himself to court you."

"Yeah, okay."

Chet winked. "Not everyone has a self-confidence chip on their shoulder, though. Some of us welcome a Hafu that the other Kind can't ignore."

I tried to match his smile. I appreciated his honesty. The Council's constant underestimation of the Eight Span Mirror Hafu in Japan gave me an inkling that the long lives of the Kind sadly hadn't given them wisdom to overcome prejudices, but I really didn't have time to worry about this Portland political snarl at the moment.

In the kitchen there was a definite lack of coffee, pancakes and bacon. Nothing for my hands to fiddle with in the face of the tension thickening the air between Ken and Kwaskwi who were facing each other like two alpha gorillas clutching coffee mugs for bashing heads.

"Egos make things tetchy," Pon-suma remarked in Japanese. I sat next to him at the round kitchen table, steering clear of the testosterone-fest at the breakfast bar.

"I'm willing to act as bait," I said in English.

"That's my brave Baku-ette," Kwaskwi said with a smirk. "*Demo Nihongo wo hanishimashou.*"

Why does he want us to speak Japanese? Everyone here but Elise and Chet were fluent.

"Koi-chan," said Ken. He acknowledged Kwaskwi by speaking in Japanese but didn't release the death-grip on his mug or his anger. "There are other ways to handle your sister's ex-boyfriend. Thunderbird could be bait."

"Thunderbird is not a weapon or a slave," said Kwaskwi. "He came last night to honor Dzunukwa, but he doesn't come when I snap my fingers."

"I understand it's dangerous," I said. "But those death and dream quotes were aimed at me. Believe me, I would love to let your loyal minions do the dirty work. But Pete...er James, whatever his name is, has it out for me. I don't think he's going to leave me and Marlin alone without one more chance to force a confrontation with the object of his obsession so he can spew hateful bigotry all over us. And if we just take him out secretly, his posse will go after me anyway since that was their leader's focus."

My little speech took the boys by surprise and the testosterone level in the room ratcheted down two notches.

Kwaskwi's eyes crinkled at the corners, making his smile genuine. "Damn girl, you're just all full of surprises."

"What?"

"Insightful villain psycho-analysis," Pon-suma observed drily.

"I feel like a proud Papa." Kwaskwi folded his arms against his chest and observed me with a proprietary air.

I rolled my eyes. "One thing has to be crystal clear. If I'm bait, then I get to decide what happens to whoever gets caught in the trap."

Kwaskwi snorted. "Has your psycho-analysis extended to the ramifications on the morale and lives of the Portland Kind if Mr. Thorvald is allowed to continue his earthly existence beyond the next twenty-four hours?"

"No murder."

"It's justice. He murdered Dzunukwa."

"And I murdered Yukiko-sama!"

Kwaskwi made a strangled sound and tugged his earlobe with one hand. He hesitated, exchanging a grim twist of the mouth with Ken, who had stiffened, holding himself and his words in check while my chest heaved liked I'd run up Mt. Tabor.

"Ah," said Kwaskwi. He cracked his knuckles. "There it is. I wondered when we'd get to this."

"That is so far from the truth," Ken said softly, so upset he switched to English as if I were more likely to believe his words in my dominant language. "Yukiko-sama chose to die. She chose to give her life energy to right a long-suffered wrong. Don't take away her dignity and sacrifice with your self-centeredness."

I sucked air between gritted teeth. My skin felt scraped raw by Ken's words, by the intensity of the emotions filling them. I plucked at my shirt and twisted my hands together on my lap. I needed chocolate or a latte or *something* to focus on, or risk upchucking Chet's pancakes all over the table.

"He's right," Kwaskwi said. "Overwrought, but right." He lightly rested a fist on the breakfast bar. "That whole Black Pearl mess is not on you. It's on the Council. On that asshole Tojo." His voice dropped to almost a whisper. "You set the ancient one free."

My throat was so tight I couldn't speak. A tear welled from my right eye and made a sticky trail down my cheek. "I ate her dream.

Me. At the end, I devoured her most intimate dream of herself until she had nothing left. And I *enjoyed* it." I titled my gaze up to see Kwaskwi's reaction to this horrible confession.

Deep melancholy shone from his brown eyes. He came over to the table and put a hand over my clothed wrist, and it felt warm, the light clasp a benediction. Then he backed away, putting his hands in the air like a holy roller. "Oh lordy, *save* me from a woman who done found out about her own power!" He speared me with a sly look. "And who *likes* it."

Point, Kwaskwi.

I cleared my throat. "I'm still adamant about the no murder thing. We catch Pete in some illegal act and give him over to the human legal system."

"Can we hurt him?" Was that glint in Kwaskwi's eyes malice or humor?

I remembered the names that bastard had called Marlin. "Sure."

"Maiming also okay?"

"Don't push it."

Kwaskwi fluttered tented fingers together in front of his face like a mad scientist in a movie. "Excellent," he said in a weird faux German accent. "This is the plan. Koi's going to go out somewhere with Pon-suma, because, face it, you're the least scary looking."

Pon-suma was nonplussed. He blinked and gave a nod. Kwaskwi continued. "Ken, you're going to put that Kitsune illusion to good use and disguise a bunch of us as innocent bystanders. We'll make sure Mr. Thorvald knows exactly how vulnerable Koi will be. He won't be able to resist a chance to assault her considering the beating he took last night. We'll go along for the ride as far as he takes it, unless Koi seems in danger of actual bodily harm."

"I know just the place," I said. "That coffee shop we went to nearby, the barista said guys with the Nordvast Uffheim tattoos hang out there."

The corner of Pon-suma's mouth quirked up. "*Yappari kou-hi kankei.*"

So...yeah, another coffee connection, sue me wolf-boy.

"That's not a usual Kind hangout. That would probably work." I could literally see the gears churning inside Kwaskwi's brain.

"How will you make sure Thorvald knows Koi will be vulnerable tonight?" Ken asked.

"Like this," said Kwaskwi. "Just play along." He switched back to English. "You're not willing to help us?" He blew an exasperated raspberry. In a louder-than-needed tone, he continued. "I should have known. You Hafu are all alike. Not willing to put skin in the game. Fine," he flounced toward the hallway, stopping in the doorway. "Run away and hide with your little Kitsune boy-toy. See where it gets you. I wash my hands of you."

He gave a big grin and dramatic wink before his expression twisted into one of righteous anger. He turned on his heel to storm out of the kitchen.

"Ah," said Pon-suma in whispered Japanese. "The traitor is Chet or Elise."

CHAPTER TWENTY-THREE

It was like he'd dumped ice water over my head. No, not Chet. He was so...nice, so normal and freshly-scrubbed. You could take him to meet your granny for tea and not worry. But that left Elise. While Morbanoid Koi was all too petty-happy to embrace Elise's betrayal on that scale, the rest of me was horrified.

How could she do that? She was part of the gang. She'd gone through a bunch of crap with Kwaskwi and even me. Wasn't she attacked herself?

It could have been staged, Morbanoid Koi pointed out. *To throw off suspicion. Maybe that's why she didn't want me poking at her hooded man dream.*

A thousand questions jostled for position in my throat, none of which I could apparently ask.

"What do we do now?" I didn't want to sit in Elise's kitchen with these suspicions darting in like piranha to tear off little pieces of my heart.

"We wait till dark," said Ken. He disappeared into the hallway, leaving Pon-suma and I to give each other uncomfortable looks. Pon-suma shook his head slowly, sitting like a statue. He often looked distracted, listening to some mesmerizing soundtrack no one else could hear but it was a mistake to believe he didn't know every detail of the situation. Times like this, though, I envied him that self-containment. Today he had his thick, wavy hair in a messy, low man-bun. The orange-dyed color was fading into a dark grey, revealing streaks of white along his temples.

Here was another person I'd assumed was around my age. But he'd been a Captain in the Japanese Occupation army in Manchuria during World War II, just like Dad. Who knew how old he was. And maybe it didn't matter. Kwaskwi didn't seem to let it faze him.

It bothered me more that Dad had hidden his long life from me than Ken did. "Is it rude to ask how old a Kind is?"

Pon-suma's eyes zeroed in on me like an artsy movie segue. "Yes. Mid-1700's."

"Hah?"

"I lived with my Horkew Kamuy mother for a long while. Time passes differently for us. Never knew my human father. By the time I was old enough to care, he was gone."

"I'm sorry."

"*Shoga nai*," said Pon-suma, shrugging. *There's nothing that can be done.*

"Can I ask another rude question?"

He shrugged again.

"Did you come to Portland just for Kwaskwi?" His cheeks turned beet red in an instant. "I mean, Ken is in the same boat, and I'm curious if you resent leaving your home and family and friends on the chance that this all might work out?"

Pon-suma hissed through closed teeth and got up, going to stick his head in the refrigerator. *Ah, guess that one was too rude even for Mr. Stoic Wolf.*

Ken returned to the kitchen, his mouth pursed together in a grim line. I wish I had the guts to ask him the same question I'd asked

Pon-suma. Not that I should be thinking about that right now, because, yeah, bait for whacko white supremacists' plans should be taking precedence. But I was the Queen of Denial, and my mind just kept shying away from all the ways tonight might go down the toilet.

With my eyes, I tried to convey to him the question I'd asked Pon-suma. *Am I worth all this? Is this Nordvast Uffheim mess enough to make you cut and run? Or will you stay?*

While Pon-suma busied himself with chopping a pepper with a bit more force than was technically warranted, Ken knelt in front of my chair. He grasped my knees, squeezing gently. His expression softened into something still grim but also tender. His overly lush eyelashes floated down over those espresso roast eyes, darkening them into slits of impenetrable black.

He gave me a beat to prepare, making his intentions clear as he took my hand in his. A flash of his forest dream came and went. It was getting so much easier to control dream fragments when I was awake, now even familiar Kind dreams as well as human ones were no big whoop. The hope that somehow he understood my wordless questions transfixed me. That this press of his lips slowly on my knuckle, and then turning my hand over to bare my palm to his mouth, and then brushing lightly over my wrist was his answer.

"Do not fear. I will protect you with all I have."

The rush of warmth traveling up my arm and straight down to my heart, making it swell uncomfortably large within my ribcage, took on a chill tinge. He thought I was scared of Nazis. Apparently, we did not share a psychic bond.

I sighed. "What's Kwaskwi's plan?"

"My plan is tonight I'm sick and tired of everyone," said Kwaskwi from the kitchen doorway. "You guys go home. There's nothing more for us to discuss. I have to consult with more of the Kind before we make our move on the Nordvast Uffheim since little scaredy-pants Baku doesn't want to help. Koi, you should probably leave Portland for a few days." He was speaking in English and waggled his eyebrows at me in a way that said this was not what he really meant.

Ken got up. "Why don't you go ahead to that Rain or Shine Café, Koi? I need to discuss what Kwaskwi's going to suggest to the rest of the Portland Kind. I'll join you in a bit."

Kwaskwi walked over to the stove and snagged a piece of glistening eggplant from Pon-suma's energetically sizzling wok. He rolled his eyes in pleasure and snagged another one. "Yeah, thanks for coming over. See you." He waved me off in a fluttering motion.

"That's it? All I get is a *see you?*"

"Koi shouldn't go alone," said Ken.

"Pon-suma can go with her."

"I'll go with her," said Chet from the doorway.

Kwaskwi frowned. That wasn't in his plan, apparently. I understood that he wasn't really sending me out for coffee alone, but I preferred Pon-suma since there was a chance the traitor was Chet. But if I protested, it would be weird. "Okay," I said to Chet cheerfully. "Let's go, then. I'm jonesing for a Lavender Latte."

He held out his elbow at a right angle like he was escorting me to a dance, and I wrapped my arm around his. There wasn't even a peep from Elise as we exited the house. The sun sat low in the sky, brushing the tops of the houses. A few cars trundled along this residential street, but there were no other pedestrians on the road—everyone was at home making dinner. I wished I was curled up in one of Mom's Hawaiian quilts, eating Dad's miso-braised eggplant and pepper and binge-watching Leverage with Marlin.

As we turned the corner, a blue jay squawked loudly from the top of an electric pole. As it took off into the ominously clouded sky, a small scrap of white fluttered to the ground. I bent over to pick it up.

It was a note.

Have an argument with Chet at the coffee shop. Stalk out of the shop alone in anger. Don't worry, we got your back.

Always showboating with the blue jays. Why couldn't Kwaskwi just text? It wasn't like he didn't have my cell number.

"Something's going on, isn't it?" Chet said, eyeing the crumpled note in my fist like he knew what it contained.

I shrugged. This was why I wanted Pon-suma. I had no idea how much to trust him, especially since Kwaskwi hadn't trusted him with the real plan.

He didn't trust me with the details of the real plan, either, actually.

"Isn't something always going on with Kwaskwi?"

"Yeah," said Chet. A wealth of complicated emotions was packed into that one word. "You hit the nail on the head."

We turned the corner on to the commercial street and the streetlights flickered on with a metallic hum. More pedestrians appeared all of a sudden. Somehow they were all white, male, tattooed, and sported beanies pulled down low on their foreheads. Portland was so white bread sometimes it made my teeth ache. Or it could be I was extra sensitive to the sight of white males.

Chet opened the Rain or Shine Café's door just as a light pattern of raindrops spotted the surrounding pavement. Inside, a few college aged girls camped out at tables in the back, their faces lit by the flickering light of their open laptops. Thankfully, the only white guys were two older gentlemen huddled over a Go board, concentrating so hard on their little black and white pebbles they didn't even look up when we entered.

White supremacists didn't play Asian board games. Relief loosened tension in my shoulders. Guilt immediately followed the relief—we were supposed to draw out the stupid white supremacists.

Chet ordered hazelnut biscotti with his flat white. I went for the organic pumpkin bread with my Lavender Latte. The barista was different today—a well-figured lady with long, gray hair caught in a hippie twist. She told us to take a seat after handing us mismatched saucers with our treats.

I steered us towards a seat by the big plate-glass window at the front. Chet flashed me a tentative smile. A low rumble of thunder vibrated the wooden table under my hands. "So," he said. "You and I are some kind of bait?"

Definitely a sharp one, here. I looked around the café and up and down the street. "Yes," I said. "But we're not going to be obvious about it."

Chet laughed. "Got it."

"Why are you so amused?"

He channeled Chandler from the TV show Friends. "Could you be more obvious? You haven't stopped scanning for danger since we left Elise's house."

I saw a series of realizations sink in. The amusement drained from his face. "Crap. It's her, isn't it?"

I tilted my head to the side. I was pretty sure it was Elise. But I couldn't verbalize it.

Chet rubbed his face vigorously. "Fool me twice, shame on me," he said softly. He took a bite of his biscotti and chewed thoughtfully. "This isn't the first time Elise has caused trouble. She doesn't care very much for the way Hafu are treated like second class Kind."

"I got that impression, yes."

"I just never..." he let that thought trail away. The barista came over with our drinks and hesitated over handing me the latte, staring curiously at my hair in a way that made me wonder if I had crazy bedhead or a giant wart.

Outside the glass, ominous clouds covered the early evening moon, and the rain pelted down in earnest. A few pedestrians huddled under the scant cover of the alleyway next to the café. Lightning flashed. The thunder came seconds later. The barista gave a little shiver and retreated behind the counter again.

Chet took a sip of his coffee, warming both hands on the mug. "Storm's here."

"Was it tough, growing up Hafu here?"

"I imagine it was something like what you experienced."

"Dad kept the Kind secret. Kept his Baku-ness secret."

"I mean, growing up bicultural," he said. "I dated a half-Vietnamese guy once. He was always having to shield me from his family. And there were like all these community activities he had to go do, and the whole language thing. It worked because I had the same issues going on—trying to keep Marigold from scaring off boyfriends."

"Wait, Marigold? I thought she was Elise's mother."

"She's my Aunt. My very opinionated, scary Aunt who probably knows I'm gay but doesn't talk about it to my parents, thankfully."

"Gotcha."

"Was that comparison too presumptuous?"

"Being bicultural in Portland isn't too much of a big deal. I mean, it sucked having to lose my Saturdays to Japanese school, and there was some elementary school teasing whenever I brought left over sushi for lunch. Mainly, like you said, it was a sense of having this whole other language and culture that bonded me to my family and other Japanese here."

Chet swallowed the last bite of his biscotti and brushed crumbs from his shirt. "That's what it was like being Kind, as well. Except that it gave me a bond to scary people like Dzunukwa as well as the nice ones like Henry and George." He frowned. "Shit. Henry."

"Yeah," I said.

"He was literally a Teddy Bear. How could anyone hate him that much?"

"I don't know," I said with a sigh. Behind me, the café door opened, letting in the musty scent of rain as well as two young guys, their black t-shirts soaked and clinging to their torsos. "Fear, maybe? Hatred of the other? All the usual reasons humanity picks on others?"

Chet mumbled something behind his mug.

"What?"

"Those guys who came in have tattoos."

I glanced at the counter and immediately felt like a doofus. It wasn't like their tattoos would be glowing swastikas. "We're supposed to get in a fight and I'm supposed to storm out alone."

Chet settled back in his chair. "Worried I'll mess things up by saying some chivalrous thing about not leaving you alone?" He laughed. "Don't worry. I'll follow Kwaskwi's master plan. I've learned the hard way it's best just to go along with him. Besides. There's a whole bevy of bedraggled blue jays settled on the dormers of the building across the street."

Blue jays made me feel better. Definitely. "I'll be fine."

"This is so cliché, but I have to say it. Be careful. Take care of yourself. Kwaskwi's trustworthy, he'll do his best not to let anything hurt you, but even he's not infallible. I think sometimes he forgets that the rest of us can't just fly away from our problems."

Thanks for the warning, but I get that, dude. Dzunukwa. Henry. "I'll be careful. But hey, before we do this, can I, I mean…would you mind if I touched your hand?"

Chet's eyes widened. "You want to, uh, eat something more than your bread?"

I nodded. Couple of smooth talkers we were. Neither of us could say it out loud—I wanted a fragment from Chet.

"It won't hurt, right?"

"No. You won't even notice."

"Will it help?"

"Maybe? It's just a hunch I have."

"Okay, although I feel like this is really intimate. Maybe we should at least go steady first."

I laughed. He was so wholesome. And nice. And I wished I had grown up knowing him and the other Portland Hafu. He rested his hand, palm up, on the table. I took in a deep breath and brushed his palm with mine. I got a flash of bleachers, and the blaring of a marching band, and the smell of teen sweat and fake turf. With as much effort as holding in a cough, I cut off the fragment. He was safe. The traitor wasn't him.

"Thanks."

Chet's placid expression had hardened. Something in his manner soured. He leaned forward, both hands slapping the table. "You always say the same damn thing, girl. I'm so sick of your bitching."

Mentally prepared as I was, it still was a bit shocking how quickly Chet was able to go from amiable guy to asshole. "Fuck you. I'll say what I want."

"Fuck you, too!"

"I'm not sitting here letting you insult me."

"Why don't you run away home, then?"

"Fine!"

"Fine!" Chet was having trouble keeping an angry expression. His eyes crinkled with mirth. The barista and her young white guy patrons were staring our direction, along with everyone else in the café. Suddenly leaving, even out into the rain, felt like an attractive escape path.

"Don't try to text me with your apology. I'm turning off my cell." The chair screeched on the concrete floor as I stood up abruptly. I strode to the door and opened it with a bang. Chilly rain instantly drenched me to the skin. Stupid plan would give me the flu. I ran for the alleyway. It was deserted now, only smashed beer cans and crumpled papers to keep me company.

Elise better have already called her Nazi friends. I am not standing out here for too long.

Thunder rumbled again, very close. I eyed the café door, needing to see the danger coming. Two more agonizing minutes passed. My phone buzzed, making me literally jump out of my skin. As I reached inside my sopping pocket, something hard and thick whacked me across the back of my head. There was a flash of lightning and a blossom of pain, and then nothing.

CHAPTER TWENTY-FOUR

My mouth felt stuffed with cotton. I tried to open my eyes and turn on the bedside lamp but something was wrapped around my face and my wrists were tangled in the sheets. I tugged, but nothing budged.

Oh. Not tangled. Bound.

I swallowed, wincing at the soreness in my throat. Dried drool made a crust along the right side of my face. I was tied up and blindfolded. Vibration at my back and the swoosh of driving rain made it clear I was traveling in a car. I strained, but couldn't hear anything but the storm.

Where is the cavalry?

Fear spiked my stomach. My head was a dull, throbbing ache. Uncomfortable awareness that I was not alone prickled my skin. *Shit.* This wasn't supposed to be happening.

"She's awake," said a male voice.

I flinched. Someone else gave a low chuckle.

"Should we thump her again?"

"Nah, he wants her conscious."

"But what if she starts messing with our heads with that Jap psychic stuff?"

"She has to be touching you, stupid."

"So he says. But what if he's wrong? What if she can reach into our minds from back there and fuck shit up?"

"Shut up, man. I'm telling you it's cool."

"But you heard Brian, man. They fucked him up. Twisted things all around. They forced him to give away—"

"Shut it." The words were bullets of compressed violence. "Put something on until we get there."

Loud, punk metal music suddenly filled the space with harsh riffs and German sounding yells. While jarring, it acted like a kind of teeth-buzzing insulation between me and the fear-grenade tick-tocking madly within my chest. They'd killed Dzunukwa and Henry. What would they do with me? Why did he, who I was guessing was Pete…or Grand Dragon James or whatever he called himself, want me awake?

Why is he obsessed with Baku?

After a million years, the car turned onto a bumpy road. I accidentally bit my tongue twice as I was flung around in the back seat. Bumpy road meant unpaved. *Not a good sign. Please please let there be jays following.* My kidnappers couldn't be stupid enough to leave my cell phone with me. I had to believe there was some way for the boys to track me.

The car came to a sudden halt, and I tumbled down into the foot well. Doors slammed open and shut. Someone pulled me roughly from the car, scraping a layer of skin off my hands on the door hinge.

Just as I managed an unsteady standing position, rude hands dragged me in a random direction. I immediately stumbled and fell, managing to twist and take the brunt of the impact on my right shoulder.

"Get up, bitch. Stop playing around."

"I can't see," I said.

"Take off the blindfold. It don't matter now. She doesn't know where the hell we are."

The blindfold was ripped away, revealing a night sky crammed with low-lying heavy clouds, tree tops, and the brightness of a thousand stars. The air had a clean, chill scent, and the chirping of crickets indicated it was night and we were somewhere out in the country. How much time had I lost while unconscious?

A guy leaned over me. Military haircut. Big, ornate words tattooed on his neck. Breath like he'd just eaten possum road kill. Maybe he could read the disdain in my eyes, because he hauled off and slapped me, wrenching my neck to the right with the force of the blow. Another cut opened on my inner cheek, trickling the taste of old pennies onto my tongue. Shock stole my words.

"That's a warning. Get moving and don't try nothing."

I stared defiantly. He frowned, straightening up to pull a huge mother of a wicked looking cross between a Bowie and a Machete knife out of a sheath at his back. He slowly brought the tip to rest at my jawline. "Get. Up."

I wanted to obey him, really I did, but fear froze every muscle in my body. A knife at my throat and my life in the hands of racist pigs. Somehow the banal reality of this, the sharp cold of the blade, the stink of the dude's breath, it made the prospect of physical harm more dire, more real. I'd never felt this kind of fear before, not with Mangasar Hayk, not with the asshole Council member Tojo, and not with any of the dreams I'd experienced. They were magical, and with that magic came a sense of the unreal, as if it couldn't really touch me in the end. But this? This was visceral and undeniable. Raindrops trickled down the guy's forehead, plopping onto my face.

I can't breathe. I can't breathe. Oh god, he's going to cut me.

"Jimbo won't give a fuck if she's a little scratched up," said the other guy.

Knife Guy smiled. I expected snaggleteeth and missing molars, but he had perfect, white movie star teeth. Somehow that was worse. The tip of the knife pressed into the flesh underneath my ear. It was a small pain, a scratch, but it galvanized me into action. I jerked to the right, flopping like a landed fish onto my stomach. Pressing my forehead into wet, pebbly dirt, I scrambled onto my knees and then up to a standing position.

Knife Guy had a shit-eating grin. His buddy had long, ratty brown hair held in place with a Make America Great Again ball cap. *His name is probably Billy Bob and his mother's also his aunt.*

Knife Guy pointed his knife up the path. "This way. You first, little piggy."

I shivered. Uncultured asshole probably didn't even get the Deliverance reference there. Or maybe he did and was trying to freak me out. But his boss *Jimbo* wanted me alive and awake.

I pretended to stumble again as I passed, stomping my foot onto his toes. "Bitch!" But the jerks were eager to get out of the rain. There were two powerful flood lights attached to the side of what looked like a well-maintained log cabin. From somewhere nearby I could hear the staticky sploshing of rain hitting water. *Did they take me back to the Sandy River?*

As we approached, the door to the cabin swung open, and a male figure, backlit by the floodlights, came out onto the wraparound porch. "Well now. Look what the cat dragged in," said a voice. This time, it was one I recognized.

James Martin Thorvald. *Jimbo.* Marlin's ex-boyfriend. Dzunukwa's and Henry's murderer, and the man who'd left those death and dream quotes specifically to snare himself a Baku.

CHAPTER TWENTY-FIVE

"Welcome to my humble abode," said James. The scars from where Marigold had burned his face were red and shiny. He looked like a psychotic pink raccoon. I hoped they still hurt.

"Yeah, for sure," I said, setting my jaw so my teeth wouldn't chatter. The lull was over, and now the weather hit with a driving mix of rain and sleet. My kidnappers moved to stand under the porch's shelter, leaving me marooned at the bottom of the steps, getting soaked. There were definitely no jays in the surrounding trees. *This isn't how it was supposed to go.* Whining that a second time just made me angry at myself for this whole mess. "What do you want?"

James scratched the back of his head. "You Kind are a bit dumber than I thought. You sure believed it was me when I texted you on your sister's phone easily enough and I thought you'd be as easy to scare off as niggers with flaming crosses and bullhorns. I didn't believe half of what my informant told me about you." He came down the steps, heedless of the instant drenching the rain gave him, plastering his blonde hair into a dark helmet. "Thought you were just a Jap like the animals my Grandpa put down in the Philippines." He raised a hand as if to cup my cheek.

Knife Guy whistled a warning and James pulled his hand back, smiling through the rivulets of water pouring down his face. "You said no touching," Knife Guy grumbled.

"But you're worse than a Jap," James continued, ignoring Knife Guy. "You're a demon. A creature out of nightmares, here to trap good folk and suck their souls dry."

Knife Guy thumped his chest with the fist still holding his knife. "Not on our watch. Blood and soil, motherfucker."

"I'm not a monster," I said. "I don't go around kidnapping and murdering people." *Except for Yukiko.*

"No, you infiltrate our city, sneak in looking all innocent, and think we're dumb enough not to notice demons making Portland unfit for our children. We won't sit back and let you take over!"

"Take over? Infiltrate?" I gave a hysterical sob. As if I hadn't been born right here at Providence St. Vincent. "Dzunukwa was here before Lewis & Clark even set foot across the Mississippi. *You* are the invaders!"

"Who are you talking about?"

"The woman you killed at the Witch's Castle."

"That old hag? She was a witch. An unnatural demon. Portland is safe from her now."

I swallowed bile. I couldn't control the chattering of my teeth. I was cold, inside and out. And more alone than I'd felt for a long, long time. James wasn't completely crazy. It was worse than that—he was a racist fanatic. "She…she…was a person. I'm a person."

"You pass as human more easily, but underneath all that is just a Cheese Nip who gets off on eating people's souls." He spun briskly and stalked back inside the cabin, calling a command to Knife Guy and his buddy over his shoulder.

I gave myself a little mental shake and tested the tightness of the ropes around my wrists for the umpteenth time. This was it. Here's where Ken would burst out from a shield of illusion to save me from whatever James the Giant Dick had in store for me inside that cabin.

But no one came. The rain poured down. I shivered.

"Inside," said Knife Guy and prodded me in the back. The knife pricked through my shirt to pierce skin. Now I was bleeding from two cuts. And probably the bump on the back of my head, but my tied hands wouldn't let me probe the ache there.

Bleeding. Survivalist Koi pointed out as I went up the stairs. *A small release of life energy.* Too bad I didn't have Mangasar Hayk's compulsion magic.

But as soon as I stepped through the doorway, I was too busy marveling at the outrageous combination of white supremacist and hunting décor to consider how I might use life energy against non-dragon foes.

Above a massive fireplace a trio of portraits—the middle Adolf Hitler but the other two unfamiliar—rained judgment down onto scattered mahogany colored couches. Bear rugs with gruesome heads attached were strewn across the floor. On the walls confederate flags, a KKK robe pinned with sleeves outstretched like an avenging angel, framed black and white portraits of cross burnings, and other paintings with symbols I recognized from my foray into the White Supremacist Interwebs made a chaotic jumble of color and hate.

There was also a flat-screen T.V. on an adjustable arm playing a March Madness game. The winning team wore the black and orange colors of the Beavers, Marlin would be thrilled. *If her sister doesn't get murdered tonight*, Morbanoid Koi pointed out.

"I'd ask you to sit, but there's no point in ruining the leather," said James with a jarringly gracious tone. "But feel free to squat on the floor. This might take a while." He stood with my kidnapper guys and spoke in a low tone. Knife Guy perched on a stool near the flat screen while the other guy disappeared into a hall beyond the fireplace. The warmth of the flickering fire was tempting, but the black bear rug in front made me think of Henry. My heart clenched inside my chest. I had to stay sharp. This wasn't a game. My trembling legs weren't going to hold up much longer, but the idea of letting James tower over me was unbearable.

James regarded me with hands on his hips and a comically evil thoughtful expression. "You are a prize. Definitely worth the trouble." He circled around me. "Just as she said, the perfect bait. Human enough to be capturable."

"Bait?" He said *she*. So, the traitor was definitely Elise. That confirmation didn't make me feel any better.

James laughed. "Did you think I wanted a Jap monster as my end game? No, you and your sister are a delightful side dish. A distraction. I'm after something bigger, and you're going to bring it here for me."

"Kwaskwi?"

James closed his eyes and shook his head as if I were a disappointing pupil. "What would I want with Chief Wahoo? The Uffheim can't use red niggers." He sat on the closest couch and folded his hands in his lap. This calm side of James was even more disturbing than the impression of a rabid Neo-Nazi he'd done as Pete.

"I'm a dream-eater. Come over here and I'll show you what that means."

"*And never wake from delicious oblivion where death lies dreaming of life's longing,*" James said. "That was the third quote I never got to use, but it's my favorite. I wanted to use it instead of that Heeb one. But it doesn't have the same impact without explanation." He stood up. "I," he said pointing to his own chest, "am death-the-interpreter. And you, Koi, will help me create the Nordvast Uffheim dream in Portland. I'll make of this city a shining beacon of Aryan Truth to all those who remain in dark ignorance about the true destiny of mankind."

I bit back a disbelieving guffaw. This was like pompous, over-dramatic Council Kind talk. What was James was getting at? It wasn't like I could spread my hands and make everyone in Portland start dreaming about the gloriousness of the Third Reich or unmask every one of Kwaskwi's people. *My people.*

James frowned at my reaction. He came just out of my bound hands' reach, relishing the way I flinched. "Enjoy yourself while you can." He flicked his hand at the picture of Hitler. I saw that below Hitler's face was a Nazi symbol: an eagle with outspread wings perched on a swastika. "Soon enough you will understand your true place."

For a moment, I pictured myself swinging bound hands into his face, and using the skin-to-skin touch to wrest a dream fragment from him. But there was no guarantee I could keep the contact long enough to eat enough dreaming to weaken him, and even if I did, there was still Knife Guy. I hesitated a beat too long, and then James spun on his heel and left the room.

I'd missed my chance.

I moved towards the nearest couch but Knife Guy growled and fingered his naked blade. I shivered and wondered how long James was going to make me wait before he put his diabolical plan in motion to create the Nordvast Uffheim dream in Portland. He'd called me bait. *Everyone wanted to cast me in that role*, Morbanoid Koi pointed out.

It wasn't Kwaskwi James was after, so then who? James didn't even mention Ken's name so it wasn't him. And he'd had Marlin in his clutches once and not gone after Dad, then, so—? What lies did Elise feed him about the Kind? Maybe she convinced him someone else, like Marigold or Kolyma, was more powerful. But James had killed the most powerful Kind besides Kwaskwi and Dad already— Dzunukwa.

Not the most powerful. The Nazi eagle. A flash of molten lava, and the seductive beauty of the powerful dreams in Thunderbird's eyes, just waiting for my Baku flame. What had Ken said in the taxi yesterday? *You're the most powerful Kind besides Thunderbird in*

Portland right now.

He was going to use me to lure Thunderbird? James was a fool if that was his plan. He was intent on calling here the one being that could help me escape. The thought of accessing the ancient one's dreams ran a chill excitement up and down my spine. Together with Thunderbird I could do anything. Who needed blue jays and a Kitsune if I could soar with the ancient eagle?

CHAPTER TWENTY-SIX

That is, if I didn't drown in Thunderbird's dreams first. A little excitement fizzled. I didn't have the greatest track record with ancient ones. Ken wasn't here to give me a primal, familiar fragment to help me handle the overwhelming power of Thunderbird's dream like he'd done when I took on Ullikemi and the Black Pearl, and I hadn't touched anyone else in days but Chet and Elise. I shuddered. There was no way I was going to use Elise's fragments, so full of fear and self-loathing.

Dad. I'd also gotten dreams from Dad. But his weird seamless grey room wasn't what I needed to withstand the full gale force power of Thunderbird, that is, assuming James' plan to deploy me as bait worked at all. Kwaskwi had folded me into his family, but I wasn't sure if Thunderbird cared enough to come just for little old me. I was a tasty morsel, but would the ancient one hear me crying out from a random cabin in the Sandy River area?

What if James was utterly deluded? What if his plan to draw Thunderbird here failed, and I bore the brunt of his frustration? I needed a Plan B. Actually, Plan A was Ken saving me, and so an alternative to Thunderbird actually showing up would be Plan C. Knife Guy squinted at his phone. He grunted and flicked off the TV. "Let's go. Jimbo's ready."

"What's ready?"

"Shut up. Move. That way."

"Come here and make me!" But Knife Guy wasn't falling for my genius plan to goad him within range of my hands. He held up his big-ass knife, letting the flickering firelight dance along its flat edge.

"As soon as Jimbo's done with you, you're going to get real cozy with the Terminator, here," he said.

Terminator? Lamest knife name, ever. He brandished the point in a get along motion toward the hall door. There was nothing gained by balking now. I might make fun of the knife's name but I respected its sharp edge. I got moving.

The hall led around to the back of the house, opening into a large, modern stainless-steel kitchen with floor to ceiling glass windows blurred with rain. It was full dark outside. Knife Guy prodded me in the back towards the gridless French doors.

Thunder rumbled from far away and the right door opened slowly, revealing a giant wooden deck lit with battery powered Tiki torches. I gasped, halting in the doorway. Five live Bald Eagles and one Golden Eagle were chained by their feet to an iron ring inset on the deck's floor. Three of them looked starved, their feathers ragged and patchy. They huddled with beaks tucked under a wing while the rain soaked them through. The other two hopped, working their wings in anger, rattling the chains. James, now in a slick green camouflage rain suit, stepped back from the far corner where he'd been turning on the last of the Tiki torches.

To my right, keeping under the roof's overhang against the wall of windows, stood a restless line of men in similar camouflage. Like hunter mannequins on display at Cabela's. Only mannequins didn't usually hold heavy chains. One had a long pole like a pool cleaner, only instead of a net it sported a thick loop of rope at the end. I'd seen that before. Tojo had used it back in Aomori when he was trying to recapture the Black Pearl.

The back of my head still ached badly, but it was the ache in my chest—a choked, fearful tightness—that took me now. This was bad. Very bad. I'd been sure there was no way he could call Thunderbird to him. But the sight of these majestic creatures cruelly reduced to bedraggled prisoners showed me for a fool.

James raised his arms, as dramatic as Kwaskwi at the funeral pyre, but I couldn't see his face under the rain hood. "Come forward demon spirit of dreams. Kneel." An eagle screamed in frustration and Knife Guy gave me a sudden push from behind. I stumbled forward, landing hard on my elbows next to the two nearest inactive eagles. They were too weak to do anything but feebly attempt to sidle away. I pushed myself up to my knees as James began speaking in German. It sounded like a litany or a prayer, and the line of men brandished their chains and called out guttural responses. I tried to stand, but Knife Guy stomped on my right calf and pain hunched me over, making the world blur for an instant. He slipped manacles around my ankles, effectively hobbling me.

I hated Knife Guy.

James' monologue built to a crescendo. My skin prickled from more than just the rain. Somehow, this German racist prayer was tapping into magic like Mangasar Hayk's compulsion. Blood welled and dripped down from the cut under my ear. James held out a palm, and someone placed a butcher's knife in it. *Terminator would be jealous.*

But then all my defensive humor drained away. Electricity was building in the air, more than just the rainstorm. He turned to face the darkness, raising his arms into the sky. "Come to us, great Eagle. Come to your True Brothers."

Lightning cracked the sky wide open, revealing Mt. Hood's symmetrical cone through the gloom. We were so close to where I knew Thunderbird lived. Now that I was outside, I could almost feel the ancient one at the edge of my consciousness.

James advanced on me and I cowered, fear bringing a sob to my throat. I wasn't just bait, I was a sacrifice. That might bring Thunderbird, but too late to save me.

Dad. Marlin. Ken. I sobbed.

"Now we will bring the eagle home. And you," he pointed the knife at my nose, "will enter its dreams. Then, you will make the eagle fulfill its true destiny as a defender of the Aryan Nation." James grabbed the listless Bald Eagle to my right, stretched it out on the deck, and chopped off its head with one stroke.

Oh god.

Cupping a hand under the pulsing blood, he wiped a streak down my right cheek, and then leaning over so I could see the manic joy in his eyes, wiped a twin streak on his own face. Kicking away the limp body, he reached for the next one. But the birds were agitated and while he struggled to evade the eagle's sharp beak to grasp its neck, I swung my hands at the back of his knee with all my might.

"Bastard. You *Bastard.*"

"Keep her still," James ordered. Two guys grabbed my elbows and roughly pulled me back while James slaughtered another Bald Eagle. When he painted a matching streak on my other cheek, he lingered, his fingers a terrible mockery of a lover's caress. The rain or the blood or the gathering hum of magic made a buffer and I couldn't pull a fragment from him during that brief chance. When he went for the Golden Eagle, I couldn't watch. Eyes squeezed shut, head bowed, I tried to stay conscious while my body ached and each thud of the butcher's knife against the deck sent my thoughts skidding off in useless whirlwinds of panic.

Finally, the terrible sounds stopped. I fluttered my eyelids, sticky with the blood of dead eagles, open to find James bestowing a blood-soaked eagle feather on each of the waiting men. Then he faced Mt. Hood again, raising his arms. He *screamed* Thunderbird's name into air shimmering with blood power from me, from the deaths of the great eagle's innocent avian cousins. The men chorused the call, and lightning answered, followed by an endless, rolling thunder.

CHAPTER TWENTY-SEVEN

"Whatever Elise told you, it was wrong. This is wrong. Thunderbird is an ancient one. Don't do this. Please, don't do this." I wasn't sure James could even hear my begging. But then it didn't matter. The thunder stilled.

The electricity in the air grew so thick that the little hairs covering my skin, inside my nose, and at the nape of my neck buzzed. A scream split the air, the rain lessened into fat droplets, and something massive blocked out the sky. Thunderbird, wings outstretched in burnished gold glory, descended to the ground in front of the deck.

"It's a trap!" I screamed. I waved my bound hands back and forth. "Get away."

Thunderbird leaned down, one gorgeous molten eye glowing as bright as a Tiki torch, drawing me in, promising warmth, power, and…

A loud pop startled me out of Thunderbird's mesmerizing gaze. A small dark spot of blood appeared high on Thunderbird's breast. Then another, and another as two of the men fired rifles, and James grunted frantic commands, prodding the hesitant men to circle closer, swinging their chains.

Thunderbird screamed, huffed up his wings, and sent his beak slicing quick as a flash through the chest of the nearest guy. The guy slid backwards, knees buckling, leaving Thunderbird's beak slicked with red.

"Now," said James. "Retreat."

The men scrambled in a comical, bumbling horde back into the house, leaving me bound and alone in the midst of a carnage of murdered eagles with an angered, screaming Thunderbird. James was last inside, bending to say in my ear as he left, "Enter its dreams. Tame it to my will. Or die."

Out of the corner of my eyes, I saw small dark shapes gathering in the trees. *The jays found me at last?* They were too late. Nothing mattered. Not whatever James had planned. Not what lurked in the house. Not the pain from my knees, soaked in blood from murdered eagles. Only this gorgeous, powerful creature that perceived a kneeling Baku, and beckoned me into ancient dreaming.

We had met three times and done this dance. I could no longer resist.

Thunderbird gave another scream and lifted into the air a few feet, hopping over the deck's railing and landing with a bone-rattling thud. His weight cracked the deck, pieces of dead eagle and two-by-fours went flying. Again, Thunderbird leaned down, turning its head sideways so that my entire field of vision was taken up with swirling gold. I whined, leaning forward, my body tingling, aching to drown in that whirlpool of power.

With the surgical precision of an Osprey spearing a salmon from a river, Thunderbird's beak sliced through the middle of the rope binding my hands. Without hesitation, I reached for the downy feathers of its cheek. Even before my fingers connected, the world spun 360 degrees.

You can taste dreaming without touch now, Survivalist observed, and then Survivalist, Morbanoid, and all the parts of me, Koi

AweoAweo Pierce, were subsumed in molten lava.

I was on fire. The pain was fierce, every cell in my body screaming in agony, but then the quality of the fire changed. Instead of scorching and consuming, it shifted into an electrifying, strengthening cocoon.

I found I had limbs, and that they were lazily swimming through liquid heat that burned and burned and would not allow any other thought other than *up*. Reaching with all the strength of my wings, I flew-swam through the dark, buried heart of the stratovolcano that the small groups of humans called Wy'east, after their chief. Using my beak to chip through a floating crust of cooled lava, I broke free, scrambling that last few feet through the upper cone until my wings had room to stretch free, and I soared, high above, shedding ash like rain, reveling in the breadth of the sky while my beating heart burned on and on inside the volcano.

This was dreaming, I knew. My constant dream of my own cycling rebirth, the child of a volcano offered to the sky. But the timbre of this dream was different, stronger, somehow. The colors more alive, the beating of my wings more vibrant, power swelling inside me that was not entirely my own—a strange sense of human in the flames of my heart, and in particular, one flame, glowing weak but steadily within the others.

Human.

I screamed into the endless night sky, and in my voice was a woman's fear.

Koi.

I was Koi. Hard upon the heels of that thought came a hunger, a ravening chasm that needed to be filled. The Baku inside me jerked awake and began to feed.

The dark sky, the molten heart of the Wy'east, the exhilarating strength of my wings, inexorably consumed by Baku flame where it changed to a raging energy filling my head, my chest, swelling my hands and feet.

Hands. Feet. Human. I am Koi Pierce.

For an instant, the image of the sky switched jerkily to blood-soaked wood, scattered with feathers. I knelt, swollen with dreaming, locked into communion with the ancient eagle and unable to move. James and his men crept out of the house with their chains and poles. I opened my mouth to yell a warning, and it became Thunderbird's scream. The world spun and spun and spun and for a long time it was all I could do to hold on to that little Baku flame of myself as Thunderbird's dreaming and power flooded me even as I had tried to eat it all.

An eternity spent spinning passed in a second. Power flowed through me, swelled my brain, crackled painfully in my fingertips. The Baku power clawed at the tightly woven bonds of my doubts. *I am a monster. I will hurt Marlin. I can't take responsibility for the entire Portland Kind. I am afraid to let Ken in my heart. I can't help Dad out of his coma.*

I can't. I can't. I can't. This power is too much!

And there was Thunderbird, ready to keep me with him, ready to ride the power of my Baku self as I tried to use the power of his dreaming. So tempting, so easy, to let myself slide back down into the fierce heat of Thunderbird's dream—forever.

There was one tough and battered sliver of Koi that would not let me dissolve into the dreaming. I had to take care of my worst human failure first: my own kernel dream. I fed on Thunderbird's dreaming, the power separating me from him, throwing me back in my own body, so that my veins raced with fire and pain.

Pain. There was blood. And life energy for the taking, my own and the poor sacrificed eagles. I breathed in that life energy, filling my lungs with damp and the smell of salted copper, and curled in on myself, willing my kernel dream, the Koi dream that was at the base of my own self, into reality.

Slowly, sterile, white walls appeared on all sides. A hospital bed swam into view, and on it, the dying form of my mother. This was the dream, the story I retold over and over to myself that defined me: the day I failed my mother. The day I left her alone rather than risk dreaming her death. The root of all my fears, all the excuses I'd made my entire adult life.

Somewhere, outside this little bubble of a dream, men yelled and Thunderbird screamed. But it was defiance and anger, not fear. That defiance resonated like a tolling bell within the bones of my body. This dream wasn't who Koi was any longer.

The world spun 360 degrees, and I was running through the cool primeval forest as Ken's Kitsune self. Again, the world spun, and I was standing in the rice paddy of Dad's childhood home, watching the sun rise as locusts buzzed a dawn chorus. Then I was undulating through the watery deeps of the Black Pearl's oceanic home, flirting with fishes. The strange house of sun and moon where Pon-suma dreamed of hundreds of infants rocking in a gentle rhythm suspended in cradles made of rope and wood. And finally, the dream that stole my breath in grief: the pure unbroken expanse of arctic white that Yukiko-sama dreamed when I ate her life.

All of this was contained within me. I was Koi, and I was a Baku, and I had eaten dreams. They were mine. The Baku flame flared incandescent, and the hospital bed, my dying mother, the failure to be strong enough to love her—it burned away into ash.

Inside an empty space of seamless grey, the ash floated like snowflakes. I looked around. I was me, Koi, with a human body and hands and feet, free of pain. Not bound by Thunderbird. I'd done it. Me. Alone, I consumed ancient dreaming and survived. I did not fall forever into Thunderbird's siren call. I was as strong as the ancient one himself.

Koi.

I turned around and there was Dad. He wore his Marinopolis sushi uniform like before.

How? Is that really you?

Would you trust me if I said it really was?

What's happening?

You know, Koi-chan.

This is where I choose a new dream. The dream of who I am as Baku.

Yes.

Why didn't you explain all this before?

Because. You wouldn't have listened. And even if you had listened, you wouldn't have understood. Some things need to be lived through, experienced, and regretted before you can move on.

From Mom's death.

Dad shook his head. *From the prison you'd made of your life.*

How do I get out of here now?

You know. Dad found himself a stool and perched on the edge. The stern expression that crinkled his eyes and furrowed his brow that I'd come to understand was his version of love flashed across his face.

There's trouble out there.

Yes, but nothing you can't live through. Dad gave a great, shuddering sigh, looking down at his slender, strong fingers. Funny how I never noticed how Ken's hands had a similar graceful shape that had seduced me from the start.

Is this goodbye forever?

Possibly.

Otoo-chan, I sobbed. I knelt in front of him and rested my cheek on his thigh.

There will be a time you will also need to rest. You will know then how to return here. But you don't need this now, my daughter. You need to return to your life. To those who need you.

The jays. Kwaskwi couldn't have been too far behind. I thought of the rifles, and the way James and his buddies didn't see the Kind as human.

Dad's eyes crinkled again, this time with something fierce and not altogether sane. *They're getting their asses kicked by Nazis. Go help.*

Then Dad was gone and I was left all alone in a grey room with an empty stool and a crumpled white sushi chef hat. I held the hat to my face for a long while, shaking.

Okay, I'm ready. A new kernel dream for a new Baku.

I called up Ken's forest dream again, running through cool ferns in a dawn awash with possibility. Sure-footed, reveling in my own vigor and strength, the taste of blood and spice filling my mouth. I burst into a clearing where *hinoki* cypress towered on all sides, sharp pine bit the inside of my nose, and the figure of a woman: strong, solid, beautiful beckoned me with open arms. That warm weight that had clicked into place when Ken gave his blood oath to me shone like a bright anchor within the woman's breast, tugging at its twin inside my ribcage with an irresistible promise of union. She was me. I was her. I went to her with tears in my eyes and wrapped my arms around her, squeezing with all the grief and pain and fear until there was nothing inside my arms at all, just me. Just Koi. Baku and human.

This is my kernel dream now.

And with that thought, the world raged and spun, this time depositing me back onto a broken deck in the rain. Thunderbird screamed overhead. Camouflaged men and others in striped track jackets tangled together in a blur of flailing arms and legs on every side. Lightening speared down from the sky again and again, setting fire to the cabin's roof. I blinked away the last bits of the dream. Someone had released me from the manacles and dragged me to the side of the deck. That someone half-crouched in a fighter's stance in front of me, wielding a wooden bat and wicked-looking claws as Knife Guy and his friend came at him from two sides.

Ken.

My heart folded in on itself in anguish.

He moved in a blur, too fast for my eyes to track as his bat deflected Terminator and he raked his claws down Knife Guy's front, ripping fabric.

"Watch out," I said, my voice a husky mess. James barreled

through the melee with a pistol in his hand. "He's got a gun."

"Koi!" Ken's attention shifted to me for an instant, and Knife Guy made Terminator flash. It hit Ken's wrist with a meaty, sickening thud. Ken screamed, a jarring eerie harmony to Thunderbird's cries, and crumpled to his knees, one arm hanging useless at his side, streaming blood.

Quick as a flash, a white wolf barreled into Knife Guy's side, throwing him to the edge of the deck where its great jaws clamped into his side, worrying and shaking him like a limp rag doll.

I tried to go to Ken, but my body was wrung out, bruised and wounded in real life. Barely managing a crawl, I got between him and James.

"You didn't tame it. Elise said you could," said James, pointing the pistol in my face. "You will try again. I can still—"

"No, you can't." I reached out and grasped his ankle above his sock line, burrowing fingers until I touched bare skin. And then I sent him to hell.

Or rather, to Thunderbird's dream of being born from the primal volcano of Mt. Hood, or Wy'east, as the Multnomah peoples called it. James' face screwed into a tight rictus of pain, the pistol clattering to the deck from suddenly nerveless hands. He crumpled to the ground beside Ken.

Ken raised his water-logged eyelashes and revealed a faint glimmer of consciousness. He hugged his arm to his chest, wound a strip of cloth around his blood-soaked forearm and then collapsed on the slick deck next to James.

A bear roared. A black bear, George, lumbered onto the remains of the deck, clearing camouflaged men left and right with carelessly mighty swipes of his paws. I released James' ankle, holding myself on hands and knees. James's eyes were closed, and his head swiveled back and forth. Even without my direct touch, he was lost to Thunderbird's volcano. George towered over the pathetic excuse for a Grand Dragon.

"No," I said, putting a palm out. "No. I've got him." And then louder, a yell powered with Thunderbird's dreams that ripped through the night with gold-edged sharpness. "I've got James! He's mine. You will stop or I will eat his soul."

Commotion died down. Camouflaged men gazed with horrified expressions at me crouched over James. Track suits resolved into Kolyma in human shape, Marigold, and several others I recognized from Broughton Bluffs. They regarded me warily as if I'd threatened them as well. "I am a Dream Eater and I have banished your Grand Dragon to a nightmare. Release your weapons or I'll do the same to you."

Thuds of dropped rifles joined the drilling rain. George roared again—a sound of triumph. And then my traitor muscles let go once and for all, and I face planted onto an unconscious Ken's sodden middle.

CHAPTER TWENTY-EIGHT

"What took you so long?" I said when I regained enough strength to do anything but breathe and mutely watch as Kwaskwi swooped down on to the deck and supervised the immediate transport of the wounded, including Ken, to Adventist Medical Center by a wildly racing Pon-suma and Chet.

Someone threw a Pendleton blanket over me—which promptly got soaked with rain, overlaying the smell of blood and singed wood with wet sheep—but everyone, even the rest of the Portland Kind hesitated to get close. Kwaskwi finally brought three other camouflaged men over, wanting me to send them into the same dream-hell as James, but I refused.

"We press charges," I said. "Kidnapping. Destruction of property. Poaching." We both glanced at where the grisly remains of the poor eagles stained the wet deck black.

Kwaskwi sighed. "Not good enough, I'm afraid."

"Please, please, please, please," MAGA hat guy was whimpering. One arm hung from his shoulder at an awkward angle and someone's claws had made red tracks across his cheeks. One eye was swollen shut and bruised purple.

"Look, you," I said, snapping my fingers underneath my surviving kidnapper's nose. I made sure the others were watching. "You will never, ever, mention Thunderbird or me again. You will not seek out the Kind. If you see one of us in public, you will walk the other way. Because," and I tried to mimic Kwaskwi's best bloodthirsty grin, "if I see you again, his jays will find where you sleep. I will come at night and enter your dreams." I waved a hand at James, laid out on the deck beside me, presided over by an unmoving and menacing George. Small muscles in James' jaw fluttered and his hands clasped and unclasped in agony. Despite the cold, his body was drenched with sweat.

The bastard was burning. And I was glad. I let the other men see that satisfaction.

"Hmmm, getting better." Kwaskwi kicked MAGA hat in the balls. He crumpled in agony. "We'll take it from here." George grinned—a look that was beyond menacing. One camouflaged man prayed, eyes shut against the monsters before him. The pungent burn of urine trickled into my nose. They deserved whatever pain Kwaskwi would inflict. But at least they would still be alive. Unlike Dzunukwa and Henry.

After that Kwaskwi put me in the backseat of the Karmann Ghia with Marigold. He left George and Kolyma at the cabin to 'clean up the mess.' But before we left, he went to a small clear place in the front yard and raised his arms to the sky. Kwaskwi sang, low in the back of his throat, and then raised the song into a yearning cry.

Thunderbird appeared, wheeling in a great circle over his head, the flapping of those mighty wings ruffling Kwaskwi's loosely bound hair. Then Kwaskwi bent his head, kneeling on the wet ground, for a long, uncomfortable time. Thunderbird gave a piercing scream that rattled my molars. The sound carved out a pit inside me, my belly welling with deep sorrow and acrid, useless bile.

The driver side door slamming startled me into a shiver that rippled up my body in uncontrollable spasms. Kwaskwi and Marigold exchanged expressions of anger and grief. Marigold turned to me with a careful mask of calm. "Will you survive?"

"Yes." I looked away, unwilling to share my own grief, but confident I would make it through this, and whatever happened to Ken. We would survive.

Kwaskwi drove at a leisurely pace down the twisting path leading from James' Nazi Cabin of Death towards what looked like a county highway. Just as he turned onto the paved road, he finally answered my question from an hour before.

"We lost you," he said, catching my eyes in the reflection of the rearview mirror. "They took us by surprise. That was unforgiveable." Beside me, Marigold held her breath, regarding me as if I had the right to send Kwaskwi to the same hell as James.

"Yeah, I forgive you. But we're even now, okay? No more debts."

Kwaskwi nodded once, grave, and then seemed to shake off the somberness. "I'm not worried. We got you hooked. You just have to survive a potluck with Kolyma's special lutefisk and you're one of us forever."

"Only if you promise less Nazis."

Marigold blinked.

Kwaskwi grinned in the rearview mirror. "Do you want to go home? It's safe now."

"Hospital," I said. "Ken."

"I figured."

Afterwards I was silent, although Kwaskwi and Marigold rehashed their attack on the Nazi Cabin of Death, he in a joking, careless manner, and her in a clipped military appraisal that I guessed was their way of processing the horribleness of what had happened. Ken and George had been near the café, under the cover of Ken's illusion, but they were stationed across the street. I learned George had basically had to sit on Ken to keep him from a suicidal solo run when James' guys surprised me in the alleyway. Kwaskwi's jays were supposed to follow, but half of them followed a second car of James' men by mistake, and the other half got caught back at Mt. Tabor providing backup as Kwaskwi had it out with Elise, getting the details of what she'd told James about me and Thunderbird.

We arrived at the hospital and, despite my protests, the intake nurse took one look and sent me off to the ER for an examination. I did get Kwaskwi's phone from him before they wheeled me into an exam room.

I inputted Marlin's number as I waited for the doctor to come tell me I was scraped and bruised and bloody but not permanently broken.

It's over. I finally texted her and then added Asian Santa and a Tori Gate emoji so she'd know it was me and not Kwaskwi.

By the time the doctor was done bandaging and asking personally invasive questions about my relationship with Kwaskwi, there was a reply from Marlin waiting on the phone.

Good.

I settled back onto the exam table, wearily happy. My sister had replied. We were not irredeemably broken. My legs were still weak, though. And I needed to find out how Ken was doing. A few moments after the doctor left, Marigold poked her head into my room.

She frowned. "I need to talk to you."

I nodded, wary. Where was Kwaskwi? Marigold was scary. Plus, she could set peoples' faces on fire.

Marigold sat on the bed next to me. Stiff. "There needs to be an apology. Unforgiveable things have been done." She made a fist.

I flinched.

Marigold stared at me in surprise. "You fear me?" She mulled this over while I surreptitiously pressed the nurse call button about ten times with my right hand. Did she blame me for everything that went down?

"I'm sorry."

"No," said Marigold. "The apology is from me. For my daughter and what she has done to the Portland Kind."

Chet walked in with Styrofoam cups of stale-smelling coffee and granola bars perched in his hands. He wore scrubs as if he were working here. Marigold looked at him, puzzled. "She's afraid of me."

Chet smiled and handed off a cup to her. "See, I told you Tante Mari, she's good people." He turned to me. "She thought you might go after Elise for revenge." He bent down and casually plugged in the other end of the loose nurse call button cable.

I snagged a granola bar from his pile, wolfing it down like it was Godiva truffles, suddenly ravenous. Pain ratcheted pins into my temples. Dream-eating blowback. The room was too bright, and the worried faces of the others too much for me to bear. I closed my eyes for a few seconds, wishing they would go away and leave me alone.

There was murmured conversation and shuffling. I opened my eyes after some deep breathing, only to see the familiar grinning face of Kwaskwi standing in the doorway with a wheelchair, Pon-suma silently gliding in behind him. "Koi."

"What do you want now?"

Kwaskwi put a hand on Marigold's shoulder. "Just making sure you didn't resort to a coma to avoid me." He gently pulled Marigold back so he could stand close to the bedside. "The Nazis wanted you for world domination." He lightly cuffed me on the shoulder. "I want to ensure you know we want you because of your bright and cheery personality." He looked deep into my eyes serious, regal and sure as if he still wore the Eagle War Bonnet from the pyre. Then he relaxed back onto his heels. "I'll take you to Ken."

"What about Elise?" Marigold protested.

"Marigold. Don't challenge me on this."

"You let the human scum live. He's in a hospital getting care. Yet you shut a beloved daughter of the Kind in a shed!"

"She must pay this time. For Dzunukwa. For Henry."

An expression of horror dawned on Marigold's face. She knelt on one knee, barely able to speak. "By the love we shared, Siwash Tyee, I ask of thee not to kill my daughter."

And the revelations kept coming. Kwaskwi certainly got around. But he wasn't swayed by her plea. "She cannot ever live in Portland or the United States again. She is damaged. She has damaged us."

Marigold bowed her head. "She's just a child, Kwaskwi. My only child."

Kwaskwi laid a palm against her cheek. "Even children can tell right from wrong, *meine liebe freundin*. I have called the Council. Tomoe-sama wants personal charge of her in Tokyo."

Marigold stood, panicked. "No, Tomoe-sama will make an example of her. She needs to solidify her power. She'll kill Elise!"

Tomoe-sama was merciless. She'd thought nothing of casual betrayal in order to achieve her goal of attaining a Council seat. But she'd also worked a long time with Eight Span Mirror, suggesting her goals went beyond just power towards a caretaking of the future of all Kind—Hafu and pure. It made a kind of ironic sense that she would decide Elise's punishment. Tomoe-san had a merciless streak and years of political experience. She'd eat Elise alive.

"They've lost their Bringer of Death. It is more likely she will be imprisoned or sentenced to a hardscrabble life, alone, in the Japanese Alps, overseen by Tengu. This is not the time nor place to make your case."

Kwaskwi gripped my clothed arms. Together with Pon-suma he got me into a wheelchair. Leaving Marigold still standing like a statue in my room, they pushed me through the hall. Suddenly exhaustion weighed me down. I yawned. It was an awfully long corridor…

I jerked awake. No longer in the wheelchair but in a hospital room. I was sitting in a reclining chair, and Ken was laid out on the bed next to me, pale and damp with sweat. But his eyes were open.

"Good morning," he said. The sun was rising, sending warm streams of yellow filtering through the cantilevered blinds. The light didn't bother me anymore. I blinked, bracing for migraine pain, but it did not materialize.

"Hi," I croaked like a frog. "You're awake."

"Sedatives don't work on me very well," he said with a rueful smile. "I wish Midori was here with her specialized pain killers."

I sat up and shifted my legs off the recliner. They were working better. I settled on the side of the bed. Ken carefully didn't move the arm underneath the covers, but brought his other, uninjured hand up to cup my cheek. Strong, elegant hands. I loved his hands. I put my hand over his, pressing his flesh into mine, letting him feel that I was in control, that I wasn't afraid of fragments any longer, and especially not his.

"I'm sorry," he said quietly. "It was torture knowing that Nazi asshole had you in his cabin. The thought of what he could do to you...I never should have agreed to that stupid plan."

Funny how everyone was apologizing to me today. "It's okay," I said, gently plucking his hand from my face and turning the palm so I could press my lips onto his warm skin. "I'm here. I'm okay. Actually, I think Thunderbird's dream did something to me. Something...good."

His breath hitched. "Koi," he started to say.

"I'm sorry, too," I said. I slowly peeled back the covers. Ken's wrist ended in a bandage covered stump.

Ah.

The moment congealed into a leaden heaviness as we both stared at where he used to have a whole hand. His other hand opened and closed. The veins on his forearm bulged.

"It's pretty ugly," he said. "My brokenness is visible on the outside now."

"Oh, Ken," I wiped away a tear from my cheek. I couldn't imagine. He'd lost a hand. Fucking Knife Guy. The well of acrid bile and sorrow in my stomach grew a little deeper.

"Kind live long lives, Koi-chan. It's rare that we go our whole lives without permanent scars. And I don't regret it. I'd do it again."

Risk his life for me. That's what he is saying.

The physical evidence of his feelings, of his true loyalty, lay starkly visceral and real against the dingy hospital sheets. The doubt that insinuated itself into my heart in Japan disappeared. Here was a man who saw me, saw the monster, and used his own flesh to shield me from the Terminator.

Enough words. They were empty shells, incapable of conveying what I'd realized in the dreaming, about who I wanted to be. About who I'd make myself be. Now that I had Kwaskwi and the Kind and Marlin was replying to texts, and I had exorcised the guilt-ghost of my dying mother. Now I knew what I wanted my last dream to be.

And two hands weren't a requirement for that. I pressed my lips to Ken's, reveling in the mobile warmth of his lips, arching into the caress of his good hand down my back. This was a good place to start.

CHAPTER TWENTY-NINE

"Where's the keys? I'll go take this stuff down to Dalip," said Ken, jerking his chin at the pile of stuff—bag-chairs, sunscreen, a cooler and a picnic basket—currently blocking the front door.

"Here," I said, flinging them his direction, and then immediately flushed red. Ken managed to catch the keys between his bandaged wrist and one hand. I kept forgetting. He kept forgetting. Living one-handed was a work in progress. Luckily Midori had sent some of her works-on-grumpy-Kitsune pain killers by express airmail. That had taken the edge off of Ken's pain. And Ben-chan was flying over next week. Having his bubbly little sister around would definitely help. She wouldn't make my mistake of hovering around him all the time, anxious to help but trying not to insinuate he *needed* it.

Work in progress.

One afternoon of work put my apartment back in order. My life was going to take longer.

As I went to the fridge to get the pan of mom's special recipe butter mochi cake I'd made for Pon-suma and Chet's team, my phone dinged. A text. From Marlin!

Nurse Jenny says Dad's IV can come out today. You should visit this evening.

He's conscious?????!!!!!!

Not completely. But he is taking food and liquids on his own.

That is good news. You'll be there?

Maybe. Asian Santa. Goldfish emoji. Poop emoji.

I smiled and sent back a perspiring smiley face. Baby steps. At least Marlin was voluntarily communicating with me.

"Koi!" Ken yelled from the bottom of the outside staircase.

I grabbed the butter mochi, the cooler, and a black silk blouse for later. After the game, Ken wanted to check out a secret, unadvertised Izakaya in Beaverton called Yuzu. Squid balls and cartilage yakitori weren't my cup of tea, but I was all for supporting Ken finding ways to assuage his food homesickness cravings here in Portland.

Ken was positively chatty once we were in the taxi. He and Dalip argued over the best route to take to Delta Park where Pon-suma and Chet's rugby team—The Portland Avalanche—were playing.

At Delta Park we lugged our stuff over to the round, green-roofed building nestled amidst a circle of fields. No one looked familiar. It was mostly women in braids and softball uniforms. Ken pointed at a group of muscled men in striped shirts with dark beards and lush, kinky hair headed to an outlying field. "They look Tongan. Or Samoan," he said. "I bet that's the other team."

I glared. "That's racist."

"Rugby is literally Tonga's national sport," said Kwaskwi. I flinched. He grinned and held out the arm not occupied with a bag chair. "Bring it in, little carp. It's good to see your lovely face." He nodded at Ken. "And you look surprisingly lovely, too."

I shrugged under his arm and let it rest against my shoulders for an awkward second. "So where do we go?"

"There." Kwaskwi pointed to the group of men standing in a flat, open green field. The dark-haired men appeared huge in contrast with the less bulky figures of the Avalanche. We made our way to the sidelines and settled our cooler, chairs, and sunscreen under Kwaskwi's amused supervision. "Why didn't you bring a tent and inflatable couch? Make yourself more comfortable."

"Ken wouldn't let me bring the tent. They make inflatable couches?"

Chet came trotting over, looking handsome and tanned in shorts that definitely revealed an appealing physique. "Hey, good to see you all."

I handed him the container of butter mochi. "For the team."

"Awesome!" He high fived me. "But actually, I wanted to invite you guys to the after party."

Kwaskwi gave a wolfish grin. "At Stag PDX? Give Koi and Ken the gay karaoke experience and see if they survive?"

Chet chuckled. "Actually, I'm hoping to talk to Ken." He gestured at Ken's arm. "You need to come in for an examination on the scar tissue soon. And I thought I might show you around and try to recruit you. There's a desperate shortage of Certified Nursing Assistants and I hear you're good with senior citizens."

"Yes, actually," said Ken. "I think I would like that."

Oh. Didn't see that coming. Ken had been an assassin for the Tokyo Council but maybe caring for others would help Ken care more for himself.

I pulled a grapefruit La Croix out of the cooler and sat in a chair.

"Got nothing stronger in there?" Kwaskwi said, settling in beside me.

I tossed him a Rogue Brewery Dead Guy Ale.

"Hmm. Should I take this personally?"

I held out my La Croix for him to bump. "To Henry," I said. Kwaskwi repeated the words and downed a long swig of the beer.

"No George today?"

Kwaskwi shook his head, leaning back in his bag-chair. He reached up behind his ear and plucked a hay straw out of thin air. Inserting it between his giant front teeth, he chewed thoughtfully.

"That's going to take a while. You should go see him, though. He likes you."

"Me? The Nordvast Uffheim killed his brother. To get at me."

Kwaskwi spit out his straw. "Shit, girl. You know better. Don't spout that nonsense." Real anger made his voice gravel. "Go see him. He has a sweet tooth to rival yours. Bring him some of that overpriced Moonstruck chocolate you like so much."

"Dagoba."

"Whatever."

"I'll go. Next Saturday."

Kwaskwi ran his hands through his hair, fluffing the ends. He opened buttons on his plaid shirt so his smooth brown chest showed through almost down to his belly button. "That's Elise's departure day. She will kneel in penance before the Portland Kind before she is banished forever."

"I told you I'm not going."

"George is going."

"If you're so worried about George, leave him alone and let him grieve!"

Kwaskwi slowly raked a burning gaze across my face. "Don't flagellate me with your guilty feelings, sweetheart." He leaned forward so his words would only be for the two of us. "I know what George needed. I gave him two of James' guys to *play* with before I handed them over to the police. That's the way a Bear Brother *grieves*."

"Look here, mister. You can't just—"

"Well howdy there," said Kwaskwi in a tone, warm as butter. A tall, fit woman with short-buzzed hair and a whistle around her neck approached. "You must be Coach Carroll."

Kwaskwi stood up to shake hands. "Pon-suma's said such lovely things about you," he continued, putting an arm around the woman's shoulders, guiding her away. "Please, let me know how I can be of any help."

Coach Carroll flashed me a puzzled look and then smiled. "Oh, Chet warned me about you, Mr. Wematin."

"Cute coaches call me Kwaskwi."

I sighed. All my irritation draining down my legs into the turf. Ken came up beside me, resting his hand on my shoulder. "Oh, now you come. Where was my backup when I needed you?"

"Getting between an upset Baku and the Siwash Tyee is not a wise idea."

I harrumphed. "You should sit, you're a little pale."

"I hate being weak," he said, but sat in Kwaskwi's vacated chair. "But there are no rain clouds in the sky. And I am here, with Herai Koi, amongst friends."

A heart string twinged in my chest. My fingers curled into my palms, aching to touch his tousled, spiked hair, to breathe in his particular cinnamon-musk smell, and stroke that warm skin. What had his life been like before that even missing an arm these simple things gave him pleasure? "And you haven't even tasted mom's butter mochi yet."

His face slid into feral Kitsune mode. I sat up, looking wildly around, sure that danger approached. My heart beat wildly. He arched an eyebrow at my reaction, his lips pressing together in a teasing, close-lipped smile that matched the dark depth of his eyes. "No. But I look forward to *tasting* many things tonight. With you."

Jerk. That made me blush right down to my toes.

CHARACTER LIST

Portland Folks
Koi Pierce, Hafu Baku Dream Eater
Marlin Pierce, more or less human
Akihito Herai, Baku Dream Eater
Kwaskwi Wematin, some kind of Blue Jay Trickster, possibly of Cree Myth

Tokyo Council of the Pacific Basin Kind
Hideki Tojo, Kitsune Fox Trickster
Yukiko, Yukionna Snow Woman
Kawano, Kappa River Demon

(Ex) Servants of the Council
Pon-suma, Hafu Horkew Kamuy White Wolf of Ainu Myth
Kennosuke Fujiwara, Hafu Kitsune Fox Trickster

Portland Kind
Dzunukwa, Flesh Eating Ogress of Kwakwaka'wakw Myth
George and Henry Gala Wakashan, Bear Brothers of Kwakwaka'wakw Myth
Marigold Fischer, Germanic Kobold Sprite
Elise Fischer, more or less human
Chet Muehler, Hafu Germanic Kobold Sprite
Kolyma, Bear Brother of the Odul Myth of Arctic Siberia

Eight Span Mirror Folks still back in Aomori, Japan
Ben Fujiwara, Kitsune Fox Trickster
Ayumu Murase, Kitsune Fox Trickster
Midori, more or less human

Ancient Ones

Thunderbird, an ancient eagle spirit most likely from Coast Salish Myth: Portland

Ullikemi, an ancient dragon spirit most likely from ancient Armenian Myth: Portland

Muduri Nitchuyhe, the Black Pearl, most likely from ancient Manchurian Tribal Myth: Aomori, Japan and now Eastern China

The Shishin, the Four Divine Beasts from ancient Chinese Myth: San Francisco

ABOUT THE AUTHOR

K. Bird Lincoln is an ESL professional and writer living on the windswept Minnesota Prairie with family and a huge addiction to frou-frou coffee. Also dark chocolate—without which, the world is a howling void. Originally from Cleveland, she has spent more years living on the edges of the Pacific Ocean than in the Midwest. Her speculative short stories are published in various online & paper publications such as *Strange Horizons*. Her medieval Japanese fantasy series, *Tiger Lily*, is available from Amazon. Her multi-cultural fantasy set in Portland, Oregon begins with the book *Dream Eater*. She also writes tasty speculative fiction reviews on Amazon and Goodreads. Check her out on Facebook, join her newsletter for chocolate and free stories, or stalk her online at kblincoln.com

Thank you for reading!

We hope you'll leave an honest review at Amazon, Goodreads, or wherever you discuss books online.

Leaving a review helps readers like you discover the books they'll love, and shows support for the author who worked so hard to create this book.

Please sign up for our newsletter for news about upcoming titles, submission opportunities, special discounts, & more.

WorldWeaverPress.com/newsletter-signup

World Weaver Press

Publishing fantasy, paranormal, and science fiction.
We believe in great storytelling.

www.WorldWeaverPress.com